The Book of Euclid
& other stories & poems

Rowan B Fortune
(editor)

GW00702896

INDEPENDENT INNOVATIVE INTERNATIONAL

Published by Cinnamon Press
Meirion House
Glan yr afon
Tanygrisiau
Blaenau Ffestiniog
Gwynedd LL41 3SU
www.cinnamonpress.com

The right of the contributors to be identified as the authors of this work has been asserted by them in accordance with the Copyright, Designs and Patent Act, 1988. © 2013
ISBN 978-1-907090-79-0
British Library Cataloguing in Publication Data. A CIP record for this book can be obtained from the British Library

Designed and typeset in Palatino and Garamond by Cinnamon Press.
Cover design by Jan Fortune from original artwork © agency dreamtime.

Cinnamon Press is represented by Inpress and by the Welsh Books Council in Wales.

Printed in Poland

Introduction

For the later Ludwig Wittgenstein language emerges from lifeworlds; those rich contexts in which the speaker operates. For children goals are immediate and not all of the received knowledge has been fully assumed. Their way of speaking can be fresh, immediate; to use a philosophical term, it is phenomenological. Jonathan Carr's 'The Dead Skipper' and Nicola Warwick's—who also has poems in the anthology—'The Moon on a String of Pearls' grasp this about first person narration of the young; these author's are not condescending to their subjects, but recognise their specific relationship to their environments and play on this for both humane humour and to say something about what it means to be human.

Patrick Riordan's winning short story, 'The Book of Euclid', develops this concern from another angle; like the novelist Kazuo Ishiguro, he is sensitive to the way clichés within the voice of the narrative encode a specific view of life that indirectly imparts a sense of character to the reader; subtly showing how the people that populate the fiction are bound to traditions and associated assumptions. His work has immediacy too; one that emerges from the material details and struggles from which also arises a unique comic sensibility about the tensions of miscommunication and the need to connect both within and between generations.

Noel Williams winning poems take yet a different concern with words as their point of departure; not in order to convey their rootedness, but to uproot them. Pieces like 'Last trip to Tynemouth' and 'Tying the kite' deploy present tense and innovative phraseology, 'Her hand pursues the kite of him/ but her hand has its own trail.' And this represents the familiar with a new vivacity, something that good poetry has in common with good philosophy, 'I used to ride./ Flinging, leaping, scribbling, grinning./ Ber-dum./ I ate destinations.'

Rowan B. Fortune
Tŷ Meirion, December 2012

Contents

Noel Williams

Silent Night

The black sky is yellow.
Siren-quiet. Silent as a mob of drunks.
LED, sodium, plasma, neon.
The domed meniscus of the city.

Through my arteries a train
bumps its coaches over glitches in the rail.
Ber-dum.
There's another on the viaduct. *Ber-dum.*

I used to ride.
Flinging, leaping, scribbling, grinning.
Ber-dum.
I ate destinations.

Turning in the sheet, tender inch by inch.
Testing my progress against
the strain of breath. Ber-dum.
And your warm dreams.

A swill of blood in my forehead.
Copper and silver spilled
by street on duvet.
Count the pieces.

Not translated from the Swedish

The black lip of the sky presses
the white lip of the sea.

She squats on bruised heels at the crucifix
of the shore, spine to the wind, preening bouquets

razor shell by shell to shred the waves' petticoat.
She winds her hair with bladderwrack, writes

a frost of salt round her throat
puts a pure nub of some stone or other in her mouth.

With bare thighs, she fills her skirt
one pebble at a time.

Last trip to Tynemouth

East seawind scoured these headstones
into Hepworths and Moores, ribbed, rutted anatomies.
We picnic in their lee, under the Priory tower
cracked against clouds like a parable.

I've cress and egg. You've Parma ham. Your hair
streams like kelp in a dragging tide.
You trace the stats on sandstone
find hints of a name that might be ours.

I snap my Braeburn's stalk, toss it,
watch it dither, harried over the cliff
buttoning myself against the flit of Easter shadows
although there's comfort somehow in the chill.

We seem to belong. Perhaps past visits with the kids
call antiphony from weary stone.
A crow lands in the lancet, black against blue.
The damp's getting through your slacks.

We harvest litter, stuff our bags. On my knees
I tuck the apple core into a grave.
The outlines of our bodies on the grass
perfect as the wind gets up.

Tying the kite

Her hand pursues the kite of him
but her hand has its own trail.
Monitoring mad paper and cane,
she's hard-rooted in the hill.

She lets out the rope,
levers the kite on a fulcrum of breath.
Tissue wings slice in the slap of noise,
whip scales of a quick, chattering tail.

Her below is his above. She barely hears
the fret of the wind wanting to rip him.
Step into the wind. Step against it.
She scours shape from thoughtless air.

Her daughters haul at her skirts,
watch love rub from her finger-tips
against the thread of their father's kite, watch
her palms bruise in bullying gale.

Their hands on their mother's must feel
the lust of the kite
flickering like a skipped stone over sunlight,
her hands unmaking knots.

The edge of the day

Everything happens in dusk.
Silk dust shawls the children
filling the goat-track with that old rhyme,
their song shuffling cows to the barn
under the shoulders of the sun.
What have I been today? What have I become?

Rooks annotate scribbled trees.
In the scrub a dog lifts its nose
to cedar smoke, squinting.
Grandmother with her peacock feather
whisks away demons, wide-eyed
at stars flaring red in the shadow of earth.

Jacci Garside

This isn't a horror

It's the Tate Modern,
a day out
after a clear scan.
And it's walking wide corridors
to discover weird art.

On a slope upwards
to another floor
a man stops me politely,
to ask if he could ask me a favour—

could he please take my photograph?
He doesn't say why but I know
and want him to say it,
but in the end I have to.

Yes, he says, *that's true,*
but it's not what you think.
I want to show someone can be beautiful
while also disfigured,
                and I blush.

I'm a professional, he says,
I'll pay you,
so I say, *yes okay*
and he takes me to various walls,
alcoves

serious poses and then
like a model on the lawn,

and I feel as much like I'm in a film
as I do when I go inside a scanner machine,
only slightly more up-beat.

Luke's Sketches
Kelvin M. Knight

Dark colours stir the tarmac and Caroline's face materialises resembling Edvard Munch's 'The Scream'.

'…That's nothing, Nathan's asthma and eczema's are so bad he's banned from Egremont swimming pool!'

'Child's play. If my little Joseph so much as sniffs a peanut, his face swells like a baboon's…'

'Arse.' Why should I hide my sarcasm? Caroline wouldn't.

The playground bullies glare. 'Is it my imagination, ladies, or did that scarecrow speak?'

Their manicured fingers flutter. Mouths cackle. Yet it is I who laugh longest for I do not wear my offspring's allergies like badges of honour, with no thought for the consequences such psychosis will cause later in life.

'Dad!'

'Oomph.' Bear hugged, I ruffle my son's curls. 'Have a good day at school?'

His head fizzes. A crumpled piece of paper is thrust at me then he zooms after a sponge football, chased by that rarest of sights: children who are not wrapped in cotton wool.

'Mr Gilchrist?' A young lady approaches. 'I'm your son's new teacher.'

Multicoloured bangles. A spangly attire. How did I not guess?

'Can we talk?' She strides away, bejewelled fingers fluttering. Upon entering her empire, she dictates, 'Take a seat.'

Outside, the playground bullies smirk as they claw their way into monstrous people carriers. My pulse races. How do they sleep at night stamping their Yeti carbon footprints across the village?

'What do you make of this?' Ms Nameless pats one of his schoolbooks.

On it is doodled a mass of crypts forming a higgledy-piggledy funeral pyre. Behind forked tongue flames, an angelic skull chuckles, makes me chuckle.

'This is no laughing matter, Mr Gilchrist, similar scenes dwarf the remainder of his books.'

'Death is part of life.' Again Caroline's bluntness comes to the

13

fore. 'In an uncertain world, it's the only dead certainty.'

Bangles clack. 'Your son needs help.'

'He hasn't mentioned this to me.'

'That's not the point, Mr Gilchrist, and you know it.'

'The point is, Ms Nameless, he's expressing himself through art.'

'You call the personification of death expression?'

'You would rather he drew cute bunny wunnies?' I take a deep breath. 'He's discovering himself through art as we encouraged.'

'Encouraged?' Her cheeks inflate. 'He's only ten.'

'A child protégé has to start somewhere.'

'Dad.' Luke barges into the classroom. 'I'm bored.'

'My sentiments exactly, son.' I drop into a sprinter's pose. 'Last one home makes dinner.'

Evenings are unbearable, mornings less so. In a haze, I concentrate on Luke's needs: making his breakfast and packed lunch. Opening the front door, I challenge, 'Last one to school...'

'Is a rotten egg?' Teetering on high heels, my neighbour shepherds an obese and wheezing Nathan into her black-hearted land cruiser.

'If they got some fresh air and exercise they might...'

'Cultivate the garden troll image?' She laughs like a hyena.

'Trowel the makeup on this morning?' I smile sweetly.

Her face is a picture. If my oils were to hand, I would capture the moment on canvas. Sprinting away, I yell, 'Catch me if you can, son!'

At the school gate, Ms Nameless signals me.

'Oh no, mate, do you think Mrs Piggy-Wiggy squealed?'

Giggling, Luke lines up for assembly.

'Mr Gilchrist, a moment of your time.'

I wave good-bye.

'Please, sir, I'm afraid we set off on the wrong foot yesterday.'

Touched by her servility, I grimace.

'You're quite a picture but you don't frighten me.'

'Yet my son does?'

Her face contorts. 'Only his sketches. Look, rather than talk about his works of art here, how about we discuss them in the White Beck tonight, say, six o'clock?'

Crazily, I find myself nodding.

14

With my back to the first cameo I painted of Caroline, I tuck Luke's creased shirt into his patchy jeans. 'Listen, mate, I want your best behaviour.'

'Why?'

'Because we're going out.'

'Why?'

'To talk with one of your teachers.'

Luke groans. 'Can't I stay here and paint?'

I sigh. 'You know I can't afford a babysitter.'

'What about our friends?' He peers under my bed. 'I'm sure we left them somewhere.' He gives me one of Caroline's cheesy winks.

Gulping, I grab his hand and hurry to the village pub. Praise be, the place is empty, save for the usual gaggle of retired farmers splashing words around their duck pond of half pint glasses. Quietly I shrink into a corner.

'Mr Gilchrist, so nice of you to come.' The velvety voice epitomises the contents of two dark pints. 'Hi, Luke, how are you?'

'Fine, Ms Beck.'

The figure-hugging turquoise blouse. The tight white jeans. My chin drops. 'Ms Beck?' I raise an eyebrow at the sign swinging outside.

She grins sheepishly. 'Please, call me Theano.' She swigs her drink. 'My parents, bless their souls, loved mythology.'

I regard my pint. 'So, priestess of Athene, how fares your marriage to Antenor?'

She downs half her pint. 'So, you know the Greek legends but do you know what's troubling your son?'

'Troubling?'

She leans forward. The scent of violets is unmistakable. They were Caroline's favourite flower. 'Why else would he draw such morbid scenes?' She beams at Luke. 'When he's such an adorable boy.'

My chest swells. I open my mouth to speak and a playground bully enters, lamenting, 'One down, one to go!'

Cheeks on fire, I stomp forward to defend our honour, only to be intercepted by Theano. 'Calm down, sir.' She steers me back to my seat. 'This is happy hour.'

'Having to endure those witches' taunts, what do I have to be happy about?'

'Me?' Theano finishes her pint then rests a pointed chin on her knuckles. 'I want to get to know you.'

'Why?'

'To find out what makes you tick.' She smiles lopsidedly.

'Why?'

'So I can help you.'

'We don't need help!' Smiling sweetly, Luke drags me away.

The morning sun caresses my forehead. I stumble into Luke's bedroom.

'Rise and shine, sleepyhead, you're late for school.'

I go to shake him, but stop on spying a picture of a black river cleaving a lady's snow-white bosom to reveal a turquoise beast with monstrous claws.

'Morning, Dad.'

'This is your best one yet, son, what's it meant to be?'

'Crap!' He snatches the picture and rips it in half.

'Get dressed,' I snap, 'we're taking this to Ms Beck.'

'You can't!'

'Oh yes I can.'

'No, you can't.' He pulls a funny face. 'Not on a Saturday!'

'In that case keep out of my sight until you explain what's going on inside your head. Understood?'

'Of course.' He buries himself under his duvet.

I bury myself in work. At midday, a rainbow-fingered thing regards me, regarding it. Not a he or a she, just it. Rubbing a sore head, I pad into Luke's bedroom. Even with his curtains drawn, greyness shreds his bed. Rolling onto his back, he presents a grey-shaded mirror full of featureless faces arced by the mother of all rainbows.

Tears brim my eyes. 'Listen, mate, it's been over a year, I think...'

'No.'

'If you won't talk to me, how about talking to Ms...'

'I don't want to talk about her!'

I lower to my haunches. 'But I might?'

He folds arms across his stomach. 'No, no, a hundred times no.'

'Okay, okay, a thousand times okay.' I hold up my hands. 'Truce?'

Tears swell his eyes. 'I'm sorry, Dad.'

16

'Me, too.'

He steps onto my feet and I waddle into the kitchen, whirring, 'How-about-a-picnic?'

'Does-not-compute,' he replies mechanically.

I quicken my pace. 'Picnic-picnic-does-compute.'

'Does-not-compute,' he whirs until I fall down and explode. When our mirth subsides, he pants, 'Brilliant idea, Dad. I'll get my bicycle.'

'Why?'

'Because you'll want to run across the countryside first.'

The majestic backdrop of Muncaster Castle weaves its usual magic. As we near our favourite picnic spot, a woman in emerald shorts and a pink leotard sporting rainbow-coloured fingernails jogs beside us.

'Afternoon, boys. May I join you?'

Luke honks away. I sprint after him. 'Only if you can catch us.' Once beside him, I grasp his saddle and use his bicycle to increase my gait, saying breathily, 'That'll sort her.'

Overtaking us, Ms Beck trills, 'Slow coaches!'

I redouble my efforts. Luke pumps his legs as though they are pistons. When we are a whisker from her, she pulls away. We repeat this cat and mouse game until my lungs burn, whereupon she gallops back.

'Thanks, boys, can I train with you again?'

I collapse beside Luke. 'Training, for, anything, special?'

Her eyes twinkle. 'Only the Muncaster Fell race.'

'Only!' Schoolboy adulation fills my voice. 'That's tougher than a triathlon.'

'More fun, too.'

'There's more to you than meets the eye, Theano.' Staring at the sweat stains underlining her petite bosom, I stutter, 'That is, what I meant was.'

'Flattery will get you everywhere.' She winks at me then glances around. 'Where's Luke?'

I net the butterflies in my stomach. 'Probably sulking.'

'Probably?' Hands on her hips, she taps her foot and studies me with a glint in her eyes. Reminded of the lovely windows to Caroline's soul, I knuckle my eyes and croak, 'No, crying is for wimps.'

She touches my shoulder. 'Everyone needs to cleanse their soul

17

once in a while.'

'That's why I paint and run.'

'And Luke?' She tilts her head.

Someone screams.

'Luke!'

I race after her again. This time déjà vu lends my ankles wings.

I approach a section of the beck where an exposed coal seam spirits the water into nighttime. I vowed never to return here, made Luke promise likewise. My heart hammers as I spot his bicycle beside the loathsome liquid.

'Son!'

Splash.

The blackness resembles quicksand, similar to when...

Lily-white limbs thrash. Eyes bulge. I stagger onward. Blackness froths, gulps, belches.

'No, I'm fit as a fiddle this time! This can't be happening again!'

'Again?'

My body jerks. 'Caroline?'

An angelic face beams, makes me whole. 'B-but, you're d-dead?' Cold hard reason recoils at the soft warmth of her touch.

'I certainly hope not.'

'What?' Ms Beck is beside me, dripping tar. 'Luke.' I leap up. My knees buckle.

'Steady,' she placates.

I fend off her vile hands.

'Everything's under control. Just relax.'

'Relax?' I force myself to stand. 'I can't lose him too!' My world spins. My vision plummets into an abyss.

Blackness peels into greyness. My true friend. I groan. 'I have no friends.'

'Unlike Caroline?'

'Yes. No.' Guilt pulps my soul. 'It was unfair she should be snatched from all her friends whilst I survived.'

'Life's a contrary mistress.'

'But it should've been me!'

'Why?' The voice is barely a whisper.

'Because it was my fault.'

'How?'

'I was not strong enough, not fit enough, not man...'

18

'Enough, Dad.' Arms hug me.

'Luke?' Aghast, I return his hug. 'You're okay!'

'I am now.'

'Now?' I study my bedroom. 'Why's it so shadowy in here?'

'Because it's nighttime, Dad.'

'How long have I been asleep?'

'Since Ms Beck left.'

'She's gone?' I try to sound casual but it feels as though the world has imploded.

'Only to the kitchen to make coffee.'

'And you don't mind?' I look solemnly at him. His head shakes. His grotesque sketches haunt me. 'You sure, mate?'

'Yes, Dad, I was wrong.'

'You were?'

He gulps. 'It's been impossible for you since.' His voice quivers. I squeeze his shoulders. 'Since, Mum, had, her…'

'Accident?'

Luke sobs. I succumb, too. Together we mourn the woman who was a lighthouse in our lives. Minutes pass. I rasp, 'We should've done this a long time ago, son.'

Bleary-eyed, he nods. In the doorway, wreathed by a fiery dawn, Ms Beck sniffs. Seeing she is still dressed in her shorts and leotard, I take the tray of mugs and biscuits from her and drape my sweatshirt over her.

'Thank you.' Her teeth chatter.

'No, thank you, Theano.' She shivers so I warm her with a hug. She blushes. 'My friends call me Thea.'

Luke rushes forward and bear hugs her. 'Thanks!'

'It was nothing.'

'No,' I rub her cold hands. 'It was everything.'

Her eyebrows ripple.

'No one has lifted a finger to help us, to condole with us, but you, dear Thea.'

Derek Sellen

'One Eye as Dark as the Night and One as Blue as the Sky'

This was a description of the eyes of Alexander the Great,
a condition now known as heterochromia iridum

I

Prurient, we ask: *Was Alexander the Great gay?*
Did he and Hephaestion…? We'd hack into
their voicemail if we could. And still not know enough.

Greatness must have been scary sometimes—
      the satrap who prostrated himself
might be an assassin, the concubine a poisoner.
He'd been with the man since the schoolroom,
had fought the way from Nile to Ganges with him
and when one was mistaken for the other, said:
      He is Alexander too.

What happened in the night is secondary.
Look into the sky-blue eye. See the reflection of a friend.

II

He'd named places as if they were his children,
twelve Alexandrias, a city for Bucephalos his horse,
cleaned his bloodied sword on maps, smearing
Europe and Asia into one, a womb of dynasties.

And now Hephaestion is gone. Alexander lies
seven hours on top of his body in tears.
      Greatness has the power
to ban music, raise shrines and a pyre of gold,
declare a man divine. But not to resurrect.

Whatever drove the engine fails. He sickens.
Look into the night-dark eye. See fields of dead. See fire.

The Road

The Tang dynasty Emperor, Xuanzong, took his daughter-in-law
as his 'favoured concubine'. After a long relationship, they had to
flee a rebellion. The soldiers in his guard mutinied during the
journey, demanding the death of the concubine, blaming her
and her family for the extravagances and corruption of the court.

On the road from Chang'an, he gave the orders they wanted,
leaving his favoured concubine there, a silk band
drawn tightly around her throat.

Returned to power, he wrote verses
exploring the eighteen gradations of grieving as assiduously
as he had explored the folds of her plumpness in the imperial bed,
(plumpness was good, back then)
paying off his son with a less favoured concubine.
The sorrows of the Emperor were like sweet exquisite rain,
washing the dust from the road back to Chang'an.

Those common men, his soldiers,
demanded the death of Beauty,
having been born unfavoured, having no heart like his.

Casanova on his Audience

Eyes at the keyhole, ears to the wall,
              they want to know
which woman's sweat was the sweetest, whose flesh
had the scent of lemons, the ripeness of a peach.

The cuckolded husband raves, his wife kneels,
one shoulder bare, her arm undulating in a plea.
I exit by the window in a nightshirt. Tales
like these I could manufacture all day.
                    They crave numbers.
How many bedded? In France, Italy, Bohemia?
'And you cared for them all?' 'I loved each,'
                  not knowing if I lie or not.

My pelvis aches like a broken heart. My sores weep.

David Batten

February

clamps the land
freezes roads
hardens everything
cattle stand in silent troops
at frozen troughs
stumped

and deep in the ice
lost faces wrapped in rags
the agony of frostbite
the tenacity
and limit of life

hauntings of Karelia
Moscow
of black heroics
an ice age away
the postcard prettiness
peeling off the negative

On the March

It deserts me:
the terror of walking a winter's ridge
under the huge stars—they inspect me,
suspect my motives—the empty air,
the aesthetic of clarity,
the blue, black, white of ice and sky,
the thrill of absolute cold, dry
seeping in through the nose under the skull,
creeping around the cooling brain
as space presses nearer and nearer
the pressure the pressure...

but now the abandoned ice shrinks back.
Drifts washed up in ditches lie defeated.
The impatient months jostle for position
to parade what they are made of,
what they can do to turn back ice,
push it to the extreme, off the planet,
bring on the green now the sun has gathered
itself to back the effort
marshalling massed ranks of humidity
to occupy the very poles themselves.

Sylvia Moody

Decisions

Events occur.
I leave home
study
go abroad.
marry a man
who has three dogs
and live in a castle.
Later we part.
I go back home
and live alone
and get a profession
and take a job.
I pretend
I decided to do those things.
Off stage I hear a laugh.

Strung Out
Janet Holst

You can hardly see the wire from ground level, only when light catches some part of it. Then you spot the silver line, a spider's thread strung thirty feet up between the two tiny platforms each side of the circus tent. Judd stands in the wings below. His eyes ache from staring up and it's a relief to flick down to the ring where the girl, Sharon, is starting her dog act. He watches the poodles tumble through hoops and dance. They jump over the pony then bounce up into a pyramid on its back. There are whistles and claps as they canter around the ring. It's a pretty act, tidy and competent. The girl throws him a brilliant smile as they sweep past him out of the ring

In the dressing room out the back, he stands leaning against the door, eyes shut, feeling again last night's weakness in his knees, when he'd frozen on the turn, his weight juggling with the air, the rope a sudden stranger, and everything crowding at him except what he had to do next. He had stayed there, breathing through it, until the feeling dropped away and he could move again. It won't bloody happen tonight, he thinks, and he opens the door and spits his fear into the cold night. From the tent come fanfares and the ringmaster's singsong tones, then a crescendo drum roll for the trapeze. He's on in ten.

He moves to the mirror and leans in close. His eyes are those of a dull stranger's. He rubs his face with a towel until it burns, dips into the makeup pot on the dressing table and smears on grease, smoothing out the lines. He drags a highlighter across his eyelids and pencils in the eyebrows. It's all about face. 'A brave face and a cool head is what's needed, Frankie.' So his dad always said. But a bright smile won't save you when the chips are down, and his father ended up doing time, one con job too many. Judd runs a stick of red over his lips, plumps them up and blots with tissue. The face now lives.

Last night Meister had come round to the van afterwards, still in his dress suit, hair swept back and no smile.

'What was going on up there, Frank?'

'What d'you mean?' Judd was towelling off and he brought the towel up over his face.

'You know what I mean. You lost your nerve.'

'Nah,' said Judd. He held the manager's gaze as he threw the towel in the corner.

'You were three minutes too long. You didn't finish the act.'

Judd pointed down at his feet. 'My shoe bloody cracked.'

'*You're* cracking, you mean. I'm not telling you again, Frank. You gotta work with Sharon.'

Judd turned away. 'I'm not doing a double, Harry. You know that, not since...'

'Marlee's gone, Frank. Get over it. It's more than a year. I heard they left the country. Gone to Europe.'

Judd took time pulling his sweater on. Meister sighed impatiently. 'There's not enough in your act, Frank. Sharon's a pro, and you know it. She's more than the dog act. Trained with her father, the best wire of all. So did you, which is why I thought you'd jump at the chance. You got a week, you hear? Work it out with Sharon, or you're out.' He paused at the door, made a gun of his fat finger, and pointed at Judd: 'Sharon!' he said, and left.

Over my dead body, Jud mutters now. He slides his arms into the cool satin of his shirt, buttons up, twisting before the mirror and smoothing the lie of the fabric. Bloody Harry. He draws in his belly. Still in shape, Frankie. Cakewalk. Piece of cake. Walk the wire.

Fifteen years. He's too old to start a new act. He's done this night after night all those years. You're only alive on the wire: everything else is just waiting. Meister wouldn't know that. How it's soul dancing—high above the dark haze of crowd, poised in the faint currents of air, foot coming forward, softly curling round the wire, balance centring. The perfection of it, *alive on the wire*.

He bends to the mirror and runs a comb across his hair so that it falls slick and black across to the side. Since Marlee went he's started coloring it. How it used to be. A fist thumps on the caravan door, and he winces.

'On in three, Frank!'

He works on some deep breathing: *in-two-three-four, out-two-three-four*. It was easy working with Marlee. They thought the same way, even though she was younger. He knew her rhythms, knew her body, exactly where her ankle would be on the half somersault for him to hold. Right at the start he knew she would be good, everything about her so smooth—bleached almost: hair, face, eyes all pale, like a sculpture in sand, her body long and slender. A

27

tough runaway girl from out of State with nothing to lose. He'd trained her and loved her. They'd built the act up in five years, and then one night she'd gone. No note left. Taken his love, his trust and gone. Taken bloody Leighton trapeze-boy, too. The swinger. He should have seen it coming.

He drops to his haunches and bounces a few times, flicks out his legs, shakes the ankles loose, clutches each knee in turn hard against his chest. He stands square to the mirror, stomach in, arms wide, breathing into the fear in his stomach. Worse was the waiting: it festered, if you let it. And then you started to doubt. She should have stayed… Let it be all right tonight.

He comes out into the lights at a skip and a run, waving towards the blackness as the crowd's roars and whistles slice the air. At the ladder he flicks his eyes up to check: the pole ready on the first platform, the chair, the safety net—frail as a hairnet from here—swaying beneath the wire.

He grabs the ladder and the drum begins the low growl, swelling, taunting, as he climbs. And suddenly he's twelve again, sitting on the low bench, staring up at the lights, his throat locked, eyes fixed on the slight figure running like a monkey up the ladder. That was thirty-five years ago and afterwards he'd gone behind to the caravan to wait for the man who'd come out with his shirt off and his braces down, smoking a cigarette, and he'd asked him excitedly, 'How do you do it, mister?' And the man had flicked the red stub off into the night and grinned. 'It's magic, lad.'

Now, as he reaches the platform, the side spots spring on, dazzling. The wire glistens, luminous and live. Half-inch braided stainless steel, 80 meters across. From the bright pinnacle he peers out into the blackness and senses the audience below craning their heads, popcorn packets forgotten on their knees. He takes the pole, 30 feet across, holds it down low and evenly spread and steps onto the wire, foot curling in the soft leather shoe, then brings his other foot forward, the pole taking the sway. He's feeling good. He's finding rhythm—breathing, steadying, weight shifting, keeping the weight centred in his chest. It's going to be all right. He does the first run, light and smooth. He does the turn. Goes back to the platform and waves. It's going well. He picks up the chair and goes out again, swings it high, places it across the wire, steps on it, steps off, swings it around his head. The act is coming smoothly, now, the confidence sliding back into his body. He gets the chair back and readies for the climax, a switch leap and three backward flips. He's on his own with no props to stop the sway. He flexes, feels the quivers in the wire, the air trembling, then steps into the bright light, blackness beyond. He moves to the middle, bouncing a little, hands holding air. He springs—both legs extended horizontally, forward and back—and does the switch midair, but he's muffed the landing, loses balance and has to drop below, has to catch the rope and swing himself up to stand again. But it's smooth and swift. It's okay.

And then it happens—he suddenly can't move. His head. Knee. Foot. Don't belong. Can't turn… cannot. Below is the net, an invitation to fall. If he drops now, he can catch the wire again. Swing up. Start again. But he can't. Can't. Do anything. Frozen.

How long, he doesn't know. Long enough to remember Marlee, the smooth feel of her, her hair floating in the airy light, the way her eyes, her lovely flanks—Long enough to remember the ease of it as a kid, running along the gate rails, laughing and backward flipping. The nights, too, in the big circus, his name in lights, the travelling. *Sky Dancer*, they called him. And now frozen here, like a fool, and gut like liquid fire.

But there's something catching the edge of his eye on the ladder. It's the Sharon girl, running up the ropes, light and easy in a blur of pink skirt and blue jacket, her legs bare, feet bare. He can't turn to watch. He feels her weight on the wire, the balancing pause. She's quick and light, with hardly any pull on the rope. Closer now. The wire tightens, trembles as she raises the pole over his head, brings it down past his chest, and he clutches it with greedy fingers, knuckles clawed, strength drained from his legs. Her arms steady him from behind, and he feels her breath in his hair, catches her smell, sweet like a baby. A moment later she's gone in a sudden drop, her hands around the wire, her legs dangling as she makes a swift pass beneath him and comes up facing him. Then she's dancing backwards on the wire, eyes laughing, taunting. *Sheer genius.* He hears the roar and whistles below.

She will never work with him, the eyes are telling him. Will not risk it. But she's not finished and now he sees the audacity of her plan. She's going to somersault forward towards him, foot-to-foot, something he's never attempted on the wire, and it will be the end of him. It's a takeover. Backward is easier, you can see the wire before you land. Forward, your arms get in the way. You can lose your head on the wire—have it slashed from your body. He watches her arms fold across her chest, the spring, the smooth wheel in the air, the legs and feet spinning, and then she's standing facing him, holding the pole again to steady them both on the bouncing wire. *The live wire.* The crowd below roars and whistles. She takes his hand, raises it high in the air and bows for the crowd. She draws him under the pole and leads him off.

Judd stands on the platform, his legs quivering, time stopped. But she's out on the wire again, now seated astride, legs outstretched. She rises, swings 180 degrees, then under the wire and over, sweet and smooth as a gymnast. She's like her father, who spurned fear and then died in the act. Judd doesn't want to see any more. He descends in the dark.

In the empty dressing room he wants to vomit, but can't. He strips off his makeup and his shirt and starts throwing things in a bag. There's a train in an hour. He'll find some small place, a gym somewhere. Maybe a school, there'll be something. He's got to leave now, before the girl comes back. He showers, dresses in jeans and a sweater and opens the door. There used to be kids waiting outside with their autograph books. Not tonight. The old silver shoes gleam faintly as he lays them on the step. He slings his bag over his shoulder and walks out into the night.

David Keyworth

Reading *The Great Gatsby* at McDonalds

I stir the ice in my diet coke,
imagine the straw is a cigarette holder,
I'm at a Long Island party
the mood music is Contralto jazz,
the French fries come in finger bowls,
a white-flannelled waiter tops up our cocktails.
I read tautly honed lines
from my *New York Times* recommended novella
to silky moon-eyed admirers.

Pale kids with bright bracelets,
bump my chair.
Still hungry, I get up to go.
A girl in a grey shirt sweeping
competition tear-offs asks
if I enjoyed my book, what it's about?
I say: 'A man who's very wealthy.'
'I wish I was,' she replies.

I leave, smiling back at her,
clutching my ticket for *Almost Famous*.
Outside the restaurant lights,
reflected in February dark,
look like the green glow
at the end of Daisy's dock.

Friday Night, Manchester Piccadilly

Staff bundle unsold morning papers
newspaper-trays become unwritten surfaces;
in Starbucks the outgoing Education Secretary
queues for an Americano to-go
behind the girl from your evening-class.
The Station Manager shakes a last dance
from lost-property office keys.
Commuters disperse.

Depot bound trains sigh through fields.
How estranged the café chairs look
beneath the queasy half-glow
their silence sinking into shadows,
waiting to be rearranged.
A cleaner dissolves the week into a bucket,
then catches any train at random,
dressed in the coat that the salesman left.

Nicola Warwick

Oriole

I take the name for bird from several languages
and toss each one into the air.

They scattered like spent plumes, swayed
and searched for thermals, drifted, little by little,

brushed my face, my limbs, until one barb stuck
in my skin and rooted. For days, I was in pin,

ugly as a squab too long hatched and fallen
from the roost, yearning for the calcium of eggshell,

nourishment of egg sac, albumen, the meatiness of yolk.
I was feather-woman, ancient and rounded,

lacking only curved bill and claw, my eyes
sharp to the distance from the stars.

Wrapped in my cloak of wings, I was tossed
back and forth through time, settling only

with a name that meant both gracious and hollow.

Think of your spine as a pearl necklace

Picture the slow unwind as the string
is lowered into the velvet of a jewellery box;
your spine as a necklace, loose in the hollow of a box,
amongst diamonds or costume jewellery, gifts
or your personal choice—earrings knotted in cheap gold chains;
the necklace of your spine, curled or strung out,
peeling bead by bead as it shifts into its pose,
support for your ribs, casket for your heart.

Crossing to Wonderland

She's found the key to the dressing-up box.
Words, trickle and tumble
down her pinafore in alphabets and anagrams.
She tries spelling her name

in different ways, lengthening
the central vowel to sound exotic
—*Alyss, Alysse, Alisse*—
Each time it ends in a hiss.

Swapping her dress for ballerina shoes
and a tutu, she hides her scabby knees
in opaque tights. *Look at me,*
she says *I'm good enough to eat.*

Balancing on a tightrope,
she stretches out her arms
so as not to fall. *Look at me,*
she says, *drink me all up.*

She won't look down. Her pale hair
shivers like a cloak. Her face
is daubed with make-up. Look at her.
She's ready to fly.

Le Mot Juste
Helen Holmes

Evie hears him before she sees him. She's fighting a losing battle with a singed porridge-pan in a sinkful of scummy water when the doorbell buzzes like a giant demented bee. Bzz, bzzz, bzzzzz!

Aunt May thunders down the stairs. 'All right, all right! Give us a chance, for the love of Michael!'

Evie hears the front door jar, then judder open. She hears Aunt May's voice, shrill and agitated, the caller's low rumble, the click of metal heel-protectors on the tiles. She hears the man's throaty laugh followed by Aunt May's cackle (rare as hens' teeth). She holds her breath. More chat, more laughter, the smell of smoke.

'Evie! Evie! Where *is* that girl, for Pete's sake?'

Evie has no idea who Pete is, but she'd like to have five minutes alone with him. She sighs, rolls her eyes and wipes her boiled hands on her apron.

'Never where she's needed,' Aunt May trills. 'That's the only certain thing.'

'Heh-heh,' goes the man.

Evie hates him. She trails into the hall. Two blue spirals of cigarette smoke twirl towards the ceiling. This strikes Evie as odd, since smoking is banned, except in the residents' lounge, and her aunt doesn't smoke. Aunt May keeps smoothing down the mackerel frizz of her hair as if she's stroking a tabby-cat perched on her head. Her cheeks are as rosy as when she's had one too many wee drams, but it's far too early for that. Evie feels a giggle gurgling up from her stomach. She puts her hand up to her mouth.

'So here you are, finally.' Aunt May sounds strangulated. She coughs and clears her throat. 'Evie, this is our new guest, Mr Collins. He's going to be staying with us for a week or so. Show him up to *Shangri-La*, would you, please, dear.'

Please? Dear? 'But I thought Mr Sullivan ... '

It's lucky that looks can't kill, or Evie would be spread-eagled on the tiles, dead eyes goggling up at the lime-green lampshade.

Mr Collins shuffles his feet. 'I wouldn't want to…'

'Not at all, not at all.'

Aunt May has another go at blasting Evie off the face of the earth, the dragon's breath of her fury scorching Evie's cheek.

'Perhaps I'm in the best position to know the score in my own establishment, Missie,' she hisses. 'Mr Sullivan was far from definite about coming back today, and he hasn't even had the courtesy to let me know one way or the other. If he turns up, you can put him in *Valhalla*.'

Evie knows she'll catch it later.

'So,' Aunt May flashes her dentures, 'can Evie give you a lift with your luggage at all, Mr Collins?'

'No necessity, thank you kindly, Mrs Daley. I travel light. I'll fetch my bag in shortly.'

'Would you like a nice cup of tea, Mr Collins, once you've settled in?'

'That would be delightful.'

Aunt May seizes the brass crinoline lady by the throat and jingles her, as though Mr Collins is too thick to work out how a bell works. 'Just give me a little tinkle when you're ready, and make yourself comfortable in the residents' lounge,' she beams. 'I'll pop the kettle on.'

Aunt May is *simpering*. Evie feels triumphant as she tramps up the stairs. She can't remember where she's come across the word, but she's sure she's got it right. She never thought she'd live to see the day when Aunt May simpered. Unlocking *Shangri-La*, a room so violently green it knocks the air out of your lungs, Evie dredges up the recital for new guests that Aunt May drilled into her the week after Mammy's funeral.

'I'm very sorry for your loss,' Aunt May had said, 'and I'll do my duty by your mammy, flibbertigibbet or not. Blood's thicker than water. Anyway, there's nowhere else for you to go. But I'm not made of money. You'll have to earn your keep.'

Evie and Mr Collins eye each other across the green expanse.

'My word!' Mr Collins coughs. 'The very height of verdancy, I do declare.' He has a slight lisp: '*verdanthy*.'

Evie tucks an unruly corkscrew of hair behind her ear, clasps her hands at her waist and plants her feet wide apart to steady herself on the dizzying carpet. She takes a deep breath and launches into the spiel, resisting the urge to lisp in sympathy.

'Breakfast between seven-thirty and eight-thirty bath by prior arrangement departure by nine a.m. sharp no re-entry before five p.m. door locked at ten p.m. sharp telephone calls by prior arrangement no visitors without prior arrangement no alcohol in the bedrooms no food no pets no smoking except in the residents' lounge where ashtrays are provided no vermin.'

Mr Collins' eyes are glued to her face while she declaims. His expression is serious, respectful, though a dimple comes and goes in his left cheek. The skin round his eyes crinkles too, but that's probably the smoke. He nods along with her, twitches aside the net curtain and flicks the remains of his cigarette through the open window when she gets to the no smoking bit.

'Porridge?'

Mr Collins blinks. 'I beg your pardon?'

'Porridge? For breakfast?'

'Oh, no thank you, Evie. Porridge fails to titillate the old taste-buds, I'm afraid.'

Evie feels another giggle bubbling up. Her hand heads for her mouth. 'I'll have the Full Irish, though.' Mr Collins winks. 'The whole menagerie, mind.'

He's no oil-painting, Evie thinks, with his jet-black slicked-back hair, his broken nose, and the chipped front tooth that snags on his lower lip. But his eyes are the green of the fragments of sea-glass she picks up on the beach and he seems to hover on the brink of laughter.

Mr Sullivan, his nose put out of joint by his relegation to *Valhalla* after all his years of loyal custom, is taking his business elsewhere. Evie privately thinks that the restful blues of *Valhalla* more than make up for *Shangri-La's* bay window and sea-view, but she can see Mr Sullivan's point. She also knows better than to stick her oar in.

'Your loss, Mr Sullivan,' she hears Aunt May say in the hall, 'your loss entirely. You won't find better than *Valhalla* in this town, I can assure you of that.'

The front door jars, judders, slams. Aunt May stomps into the kitchen.

'Plenty more where *that* came from,' she says, clattering crockery at random. 'Common little man. Travelling salesman, indeed. Glorified tinker, more like, peddling tat out of a suitcase. Don't just stand there catching flies, Evie. Go see if Mr Collins would like more toast. Now there's a proper gentleman. Insurance is a respectable profession, so it is.'

In the dining-room, the proper gentleman's pen is poised over the Times crossword, his reading glasses teetering on the end of his crooked nose. He looks up. The dimple appears.

'Would you like more toast, sir?' Evie asks.

'Thank you, no, Evie. I've had an ample sufficiency. Kindly convey my heartfelt compliments to the chef.' Amusement ripples over his face.

Evie can't help smiling back. 'Mr Collins?'

'Young lady?'

'What's insurance exactly?'

'Aha! I deduce from that question that your estimable aunt has revealed the means by which I keep body and soul together.'

'You've no need to worry, sir. She says it's respectable.'

'Well now, that's an enormous weight off my mind, Evie. Magnificent woman that she is, your aunt strikes me as being powerful difficult to impress. No dictionary in this fine establishment, then?'

'There might be one in Aunt May's room, sir, but I'm not allowed in there.'

'It's undeniable that your aunt, though indubitably a kind and charitable soul (witness the incomparable bounty of her Full Irish), exhibits a doughty façade.'

'Doughty, sir?'

'Determined, unflinching.'

'And that other word?'

'Façade? Appearance, illusion. I see that I shall have to speak more plainly, Evie, or our every conversation is destined to turn into a vocabulary lesson.'

'I like learning new words.'

'And I shall be happy to oblige, dear girl, of course, when my time's my own.' Mr Collins refolds his paper, squints at his watch, takes off his glasses and pushes himself to his feet. 'But a man of leisure I am not, and I must venture out forthwith if the ravening wolf is to be repelled from the door.'

'So insurance is—'

'Insurance, persistent minx, provides a guarantee of compensation for specified loss, damage, illness or death in return for the payment of a premium.'

'So…'

'So if your aunt, say…'

'Has Aunt May got insurance?'

39

'This is a hypothetical… a made-up example, Evie. But *if* she had, and someone stole her diamond tiara…'

·'What's a tiara?'

The dimple appears. 'An ornamental hair-band. So, should your aunt invest in a diamond tiara, then have it stolen, she could claim money from the insurance company to replace it. And now, Miss Curiosity, I really must fly, or I'll be late for my first appointment.'

Mr Collins is a neat man, for which Evie is thankful. In spite of all the rules, some guests leave their rooms like 'middens' (Aunt May's word, but Evie gets the gist): clothes strewn over furniture, cigarette stubs in the sink, bottles and other unspeakables under the bed, half-gnawed sandwiches, festering apple-cores. She's seen some shocking sights. She straightens things up as best she can and doesn't snitch unless it's something serious (like the pair of white rats in the wardrobe that time), but woe betide a wayward guest if Aunt May nabs him first. He's out the door before he can stammer s-second chance. And every time a fresh crime is committed, Evie has another rule to add to her litany.

Mr Collins tidies his room, folds back his bedclothes and opens the window wide before he comes down for his Full Irish with all the trimmings. Straight after breakfast he's away in his shiny black car insuring people. Business must be booming; he's been here two weeks already. When *Valhalla*'s empty, Aunt May settles down with him in front of the television in the residents' lounge of an evening.

'A gentleman deserves a bit of civilised company,' she says to Evie, 'after a hard day's work.'

Evie tries to look down in the mouth, but secretly she's thrilled. She can read without fear of interruption from her aunt, who for some reason can't bear to see her with 'her nose stuck in a book' and is a past master at dreaming up jobs for her: cleaning clean silver, or polishing polished furniture, or re-lining drawers. At nine o'clock sharp, Evie has to carry into the lounge a tray with two mugs of cocoa and a plate of digestive biscuits. Tonight the television is mute. On the screen a fat old man and a deranged-looking woman are bellowing silently at each other. There's a slew of papers on the coffee-table. Mr Collins is in full spate.

'Of course,' he's saying, 'you're in the pink.'

Aunt May is indeed pink, Evie thinks, but both bars of the fire are on, which would account for it.

'In your prime,' Mr Collins goes on. 'No medical counter-indications. And when the policy matures, just think of that lovely little nest-egg waiting for you.'

Mr Collins glances up at Evie and winks the eye Aunt May can't see.

'You and Evie could do a spot of globe-trotting,' he says.

Aunt May frowns.

'Or you could buy a car,' he says.

Aunt May looks unmoved.

'Or just shut up shop and put your feet up for a bit. Treat yourself to a well-earned rest.'

Now the suggestion of a smile takes the chill off Aunt May's expression. She reaches for her cocoa. 'Close the door behind you, will you, Evie, dear,' she says. 'That draught's after scything us off at the ankles.'

'Central heating!' Mr Collins warms to his subject. 'The height of luxury! The world,' Evie hears him say, as she pulls the door to, 'will be your oyster, my dear Mrs Daley.' '*Oythter*'.

As Evie settles down again at the kitchen table with her library book, the thought floats into her mind that, with her lovely little nest-egg, Aunt May could probably afford a diamond tiara, though the thought of a sparkling ornamental hair-band buried in that frizz makes her giggle.

'Pastures new, Evie, pastures new,' Mr Collins sighs after breakfast one morning, 'the curse of the peripatetic (wandering) representative (salesman in this context). Head Office has spoken. I have relished our conversations, my dear. And your vocabulary is coming on in leaps and bounds. At this rate, you'll be a veritable (real) wordsmith in no time at all. I hope that we may renew our acquaintance one day.' He shakes her hand. 'Farewell for the present.'

Evie glumly prepares the bedrooms for new residents. In *Shangri-La*, she finds on the chest of drawers a parcel neatly wrapped in brown paper and secured with string. She is taken aback to see her own name scrawled in a confident hand. In her own bedroom, she picks at the string, unknots it and winds it carefully round her fingers. She folds back the paper to reveal a Collins Concise English Dictionary. There is no note.

41

*

Two months after Aunt May's funeral, the door-bell buzzes like an enraged hornet. Evie hurtles downstairs, forgetting to peel off her rubber gloves. She yanks open the front door.

'Mr Collins!'

The skin round the sea-glass eyes is a little more crinkled and bruised; a few threads of silver mitigate the dense blackness of the hair. The dimple puts in an appearance. Mr Collins holds out his hand.

'How are you, Evie? I'm very sorry for your loss.' *Thorry.*

Evie holds out a bright orange hand. 'God, sorry!' She rips off her glove, wipes her hand on her apron and shakes his hand. 'But how did you know?'

'Oh, it's a small world, Evie, the insurance community, a very small world. I'd like to come in, if I may.'

Evie closes her mouth and remembers her manners. She steps back into the hall. 'Of course. I'm so sorry. I'm a bit discombobulated. It's great to see you. I'm afraid *Shangri-La's* taken from tomorrow for a week, but *Valhalla's* available until Thursday, if that's any help. It hasn't got the bay-window or the sea-view, but it's significantly less… verdant.'

Mr Collins grins. The chipped tooth snags on his lip. 'It's all right, Evie, I'm not after accommodation. I've an appointment over by Dungarvan this afternoon, and several down Ardmore way tomorrow. I won't keep you long, but since I was in the vicinity, I thought I'd call and pay my respects.'

'That's very good of you. You'll take a cup of tea?'

'A cup of tea would be just the ticket.'

'Make yourself comfortable in the lounge. I'll get the kettle on.'

When Evie returns with a loaded tray, Mr Collins looks at home in his old place on the settee. On the coffee-table in front of him is a large brown envelope. He slides it along to clear a space for the tray. Evie puts a plate piled high with chocolate digestive biscuits within reaching-distance.

Mr Collins shakes his head. 'Poor Mrs Daley,' he says. 'Who would have thought it? She seemed so indomitable.' He glances at her, his dimple awaiting instructions. 'Fighting fit, one might say.'

Evie's hand creeps towards her mouth.

'What was it? Heart?'

'A massive stroke, the doctor said. I just thought she'd snoozed off in front of the telly, which she often did. It was only when I couldn't rouse her at bedtime that I realised something was drastically wrong.'

'It must have been a dreadful shock.'

Evie nods.

Mr Collins sips his tea and solemnly inspects the underside of his biscuit before taking a bite. 'I see standards have risen,' he says. 'Business is thriving, I take it.'

'Oh, you know, I'm keeping body and soul together,' Evie says, 'and the ravening wolf at bay.'

Mr Collins laughs his hoarse laugh. 'Extracting the Michael now, are we, young lady? You'd be astonished how impressed the punters are by a bit of purple prose. It makes them think you're a superior being. After a while it sticks. I remember Mammy saying "Don't pull faces, son. The wind'll change and you'll get stuck like that." I should have listened to her.'

'Aunt May used to say that, too.'

'And you didn't listen either?'

'Of course not.'

'How did you come to live with your aunt, Evie? I never did find out.'

Evie tells Mr Collins about Da's desertion, Mammy's long illness.

'I'm so sorry,' Mr Collins says.

'That was aeons ago.'

Evie had no idea that so many words were dammed up behind her teeth. What starts as a trickle becomes a stream, a torrent, a Niagara. She tells him about Aunt May's draconian régime, her meanness of spirit, her bitter, pointless feuds: with the priest over the flower rota, the baker over his bill, the doctor over his advice.

Evie tells him about her own solitary rambles along the coast, the rock pools teeming with secret life, the sanderlings skittering along the shore like wind-up toys, the shark's egg she found one stormy evening, her collections of sea-glass and cowries. She tells him about the books she has read, the writers she admires, the characters she loves and loathes. She tells him how she trained herself to purge her mind of porridge-pots and unmentionables under the bed and rats in the wardrobe, how she metamorphosed into a love-sick governess, a beautiful spoilt young English lady, an American heiress. She tells him some of her favourite words: serendipity, avuncular, deliquescence.

Evie had forgotten what a good listener he is. His sea-glass eyes rest quietly on her face; he nods, shakes his head, smiles in all the right places. His expression shifts from concern to sympathy to encouragement. When Evie stops talking, she's panting slightly.

Mr Collins says nothing for a while. He seems a little winded himself. Then he says 'I'm proud of you, Evie. You are a veritable wordsmith.'

Evie blushes. 'Your turn now,' she says. 'No, wait!' She grabs the tray and rushes out, returning with fresh tea and another plate of chocolate digestives. She pours tea for them both, and puts the plate of biscuits next to her mentor's cup and saucer.

'Now you spill the beans,' she says.

Mr Collins takes a biscuit, munches it ruminatively, and licks his fingers and thumb. He sighs and his eyes slide away from Evie's for the first time. 'I don't know if...'

Evie frowns. 'But I've told you all my secrets.'

Mr Collins laughs. 'Still a persistent minx, aren't you, young lady?'

He hesitates for a moment, then leans forward and begins to talk. He tells her about his wife's death in childbirth, followed by his tiny, beautiful, fragile daughter's two days later. He clears his throat. 'She would have been a few years younger than you.'

'I'm so sorry,' Evie says.

'That was aeons ago, too.'

Mr Collins tells Evie about a ramshackle cottage at the end of a pot-holed track. A farming family had failed to respond to the company's letters about missed payments. He made suggestions, none of which the family could come close to affording. Much later, he heard the farm had burnt to the ground. He hoped they'd found another insurer.

Mr Collins tells Evie about a wake in the Wicklow Mountains, the hillsides flushed with heather and murmuring with bees. As dusk washed the sky ultramarine, a singer began to sing old songs. The pure, clear notes trilling from the woman's throat made the hairs on the back of his neck stand on end. The faces of the family, lean and hard as granite hewn from the mountains, were streaked with silent tears.

Mr Collins tells Evie about a banker's villa, stuccoed with frills and furbelows and glinting with gold leaf. The wife's jewellery had been stolen, but she couldn't call to mind exactly what was missing in order to compile an inventory. 'Did I have one sapphire ring or two, darling?' she asked her husband. 'I really can't remember. Can you?'

'He couldn't, I take it.' Evie says.

'Good God, no. Of negligible consequence, a sapphire ring, in that household.'

They sit quietly for a time, the only sound the ticking of the mantelpiece clock. Evie smiles at Mr Collins. 'Thank you for taking me somewhere different,' she says.

Mr Collins smiles back. 'Thank you for coming with me.' He glances at his watch. 'Sadly, refreshing as it is to be in such congenial company, my dear Evie, I must wend my weary way.' He gets to his feet.

'Of course you must,' Evie says. 'A man of leisure you are not.'

'Heh-heh.' Mr Collins takes a business card out of his pocket and hands it to her. She sees that his name is William.

'If I can be of the slightest assistance to you in navigating life's highway,' he says, 'please don't hesitate to call me.'

'I won't,' Evie says.

Mr Collins hoists his eyebrows. 'You won't?'

Evie laughs. 'I mean I won't hesitate. And don't you be a stranger, either.'

'I promise.'

Out in the hall, they shake hands. Evie wrestles the door open.

'You really should get something done about that, you know,' Mr Collins says. 'It just needs planning, for heaven's sake. It's not very welcoming for a body to have to battle his way in and out. And if you do nothing else, for the love of God get that hideous bedroom redecorated. It's like sleeping in the Amazon rain-forest. I used to have a recurrent nightmare about being savaged by a crocodile.'

Evie laughs. 'D'you think I'm made of money, Mr Collins?'

'You didn't stumble across that diamond tiara, then?'

'No,' Evie says, 'but at least I know what one is now. Tiara was the first word I looked up in that dictionary you so kindly left for me. Insurance was the second. Just to check you weren't pulling my leg. I trusted you after that. That old dictionary's been so well thumbed, it's falling apart.'

'Treat yourself to a new one, dear girl, and hang the expense.'

Mr Collins walks down the path and climbs into a black car a little larger and shinier than the one Evie remembers. He raises his hand in salute and drives away.

Evie goes back into the lounge to collect the tray and notices that Mr Collins has left his envelope on the coffee-table. Picking it up, she sees that it is addressed to her. Intrigued, she opens it. Inside she finds a letter from the insurance company and a substantial cheque. The letter explains that Evie is the beneficiary of Aunt May's life-insurance policy. She goes upstairs and, standing in the doorway of *Shangri-La*, she wonders what colour-scheme Mr Collins might prefer.

Kayley Roberts

Gwlad Beirdd a Chantorion

Look closer. A harp plays
in resonance with the wind, swirling
notes around the nooks and knots
of trees that once stood in time.
Grass roots that spread for miles,
Sir Fôn to Morgannwg, bristle
in a B# harmony. Even the clouds
seem to be shaped from song.
A vibrato shakes the air, blurring
the horizon and the thin gap between
reality and metaphor. Language threads
through each string, released by
a pluck so that each word
is spoken in a melody.

Interrogation

Taking into account the nature of the crime and the obscurity
of the object stolen, let us assume then that the people who
claim ownership are in fact—nobody. Who can grasp this
thing? It cannot be touched, nor owned directly.
Who could steal nothing, or lay claim to air? It is just as
impossible to claim ownership of language, words spoken and
lost through an accident or misplacement. Blame cannot be cast
on an individual. Speech must be contained securely,
between tongue and cheek, if it is to be stored correctly over time.

Poethni

Thomas laps tentatively
    a precursor,
    a tongue too soft.
Poethni.
The hotness thrills him,
    a liquid that scorches
    his parched throat.
Through gritted teeth
    he bears a new sound
hollow at first, then filled
with unexpected vowels.
Disgynodd,
      twisting
this new feeling
around his moistened lips
      he learns
how to express distance
with his native ears
and a foreign tongue.

The Dead Poet Speaks

I remember the land, the people, choirs
that rose
out on the hillsides. I heard them die,
the voices hide, the still night carries nothing.

I gauge the land but now there's nothing.
The faded language lounges at the gate
—'I'll go no further'.

I used to be a poet, flock to me and listen,
the old tales are here, still waiting to be told.
Will you hear them?
Bait for the long dead
where they piece together fragments of the past.

No use to you now.

I'll sit and wait, my voice held
between time, place, good intentions.
Let the small hands gather up the rest
and drape my chair in black.

Vigilante
Sarah Hegarty

On the day in April that Ben's headship is confirmed, two blackbirds appear in the back garden. Madeleine, who has forgotten the bird facts Ben used to tell her, doesn't understand what they're doing. But she recognises frantic activity.

The male hurries across the narrow lawn, or swoops past the window to perch on the fence, his tail up. The dull-coloured female forages in the flower bed, her beak stuffed with scraps. When Madeleine realises they are building a nest, their shared purpose makes her anxious. She can't help watching, her attention wandering from the proof pages she is correcting.

Curious about the nest she ventures outside in the cold wind, and catches sight of her reflection in the French window. In her tracksuit bottoms and baggy sweater she looks like the no-hope contestant on a daytime TV show.

That evening Ben has a late meeting. Standing at the sink, scraping the brown skin of scrambled egg from the milk pan, Madeleine sees the female bird, still busy in the evening light. Feeling only slightly foolish she says into the window pane, 'Watch out, girl! When the chicks come along, you'll be stuck on the nest!' She can't resist banging on the glass in warning, and the bird takes off, complaining.

But her words make her feel a fraud. She got what she wanted. It's just that now there's too much time to think.

Her friend Clare calls on the land line. Half-way through their conversation Madeleine's mobile, on the table next to her, buzzes with a new text. Ben's been delayed, is staying over with a colleague.

'How many times now?' says Clare.

'I trust my husband,' Madeleine says, conscious of how priggish she sounds. A small, icy hand grips her heart.

'You don't have to confront him.' Clare is exasperated. 'Just investigate. You're not devious enough.'

'You don't know how devious I am.' She didn't mean to say that.

They celebrate Ben's promotion a few evenings later, at their favourite Italian. Madeleine has dug out the faithful tunic dress that hides the bulges from her desk-bound days, and made up her eyes and mouth.

She breaks off a piece of ciabatta. The words she needs won't come. 'I wonder how the twins are getting on at uni,' she tries.

'The twins are getting on with their lives,' Ben says. His slim fingers dunk bread in a small puddle of olive oil. He has barely put on weight over the years; despite being ten years older than Madeleine, his thick hair is only now starting to grey.

'The house is always so quiet after the holidays.'

'You could go back to work,' he says. 'There are never enough teachers.'

Madeleine thinks of the proof pages littering her desk, and the regular—if small—sums that appear on the joint account statements. She tries to smile. 'But I do work. And you always said, "Never go back". Remember?'

He shrugs. 'Did I?'

It wasn't just me, she wants to say. She used to sense a bubble of complicity, surrounding them. But now she feels a tear in the skin; another world, pushing in. She can't stop a surge of panic in her chest.

Into her head flashes an image of the nesting birds. His old interest. As soon as she says the words they feel too desperate, but she can't stop.

'The nest's in the wrong place,' she persists. 'It's on the ivy, too close to the house. They'll abandon the chicks. Or a cat will get them.'

Ben looks up from his osso buco. 'They always build in stupid places.' He spears a piece of meat. 'They're known for it.'

Madeleine is horrified to feel her eyes sting. She forces down a forkful of risotto. She wants to ask if pairs mate for life, but everything means something else. She wants to press, to prod: to say, Do you ever think about those days? But she can't find the words. And if she did, something would shatter.

Ben laughs. 'You need to get out more, as the girls would say.'

She hears his annoyance. 'Maybe I do.'

'You certainly look like a home-worker, in that dress.'

Back home, in bed, he pulls her to him. But Madeleine sees his unwillingness, his wish to be somewhere else.

'I'm not really in the mood.' She moves away, and sits on the edge of the bed.

'It's probably your hormones.' Ben lies on his back, staring at the ceiling.

She waits a beat. 'What are you thinking?'

'Nothing,' he says. 'Why don't you make an appointment with the GP?' He turns over to go to sleep.

'Who is she?' Madeleine wants to ask. 'Is she young?'

He leaves early the next morning.

He has always taught in all-girls' schools. The discipline is better without boys, he says. Now Madeleine thinks he didn't want to be reminded. Promotion has pushed him up the management structure: he comes home late three or four nights a week. There is a weekend course in the offing. He has volunteered for a staff student committee, looking at ways to fundraise.

These are the facts, he says. Her facts seem to lose their certainty around Ben. He says a lifetime of teaching history has given him a highly developed sense of what's relevant.

Perhaps it's her: it is hard to remember, nearly twenty years later, where she began and ended. Her memories slip and slide, although the undercurrent is still there; the feeling she thought had faded. As if it has lain dormant all this time, only to erupt into the now-empty house, catching her unawares.

Before she starts work Madeleine does her domestic tidying and sorting, although there's little to do now. It's a hangover from when the girls lived at home—the vain attempt to subdue the tidal wave of tasks that threatened to overwhelm.

In the bathroom she stares into the mirror and grimaces, touching the fine, criss-crossed lines that bloom beside her eyes. She pushes her fingers back and up, making the skin taut, and views her younger self.

Without warning she's back in the staff room, with its battered chairs and lingering scent of cigarettes; golden September light falling through the high windows. The feeling that anything is possible.

Ben introduced himself on her first day. 'Allow me to show you the ropes,' he said. His dark hair was a little too long; his jacket well cut. She heard one of the women laugh theatrically, and felt flattered. Without hesitating he took her arm and guided her round the large, square room, pointing out the outsized timetable pinned to the wall; favourite chairs that must never be taken.

Someone muttered something she couldn't catch.

When he asked her to supper at his home, it never occurred to her not to go. He called her, 'My new colleague': said she was 'fresh from teacher training – and all alone in a strange town.'

Later that term, as if to clear the way for their adventure, he found a better job and handed in his notice. His timing was perfect.

They were adults: not responsible for anyone else's happiness. Madeleine avoided the staff room though. She knew her colleagues thought her as immature as the students. She didn't expect them to understand. She briefly considered buying herself a cheap ring, then realised that would change nothing.

But she had to be sure. And how can she regret the girls?

When they're home, they argue—with each other and with her —and the house resonates with slammed doors. Madeleine seems to have lost all her powers of persuasion.

Sometimes she wonders if they absorbed something in the womb. But she was so careful, when she was pregnant: she kept calm; held her breath. She waited him out. In the end, she was rewarded.

When the twins arrived Ben liked his new status as the only man in the house. Madeleine dared to relax.

'A rose among thorns,' said his mother, up from Kent. 'Fancy you producing girls!' She ignored Madeleine. 'I believe in keeping in touch, for the children's sake,' she said.

'Don't do it for my sake,' Madeleine wanted to say. But she bit her tongue.

Ben was involved with the girls when they were small—bottle feeds, bedtime stories, kite-flying in the park—although sometimes Madeleine caught him studying them, in a distant way, and felt a niggling doubt.

But he gave them whatever they wanted. She wondered if it was to compensate. She presumed he'd been fair: the financial arrangements were none of her business. Everything was done differently in those days. And having twins made it all more difficult. The house just wasn't big enough for visitors.

Outside the window, the April garden is still half asleep. The cold spring has delayed the blossoms; daffodils waver in the flower beds, which are full of the dead leaves that Madeleine intended to sweep up last autumn.

The blackbirds peck in the borders, hop across the garden, heads down. Madeleine watches them flying backwards and forwards, worms dangling from their beaks, and thinks of the girls in their high chairs.

When they were small she never left them with anyone. She was unnerved by how strongly she felt about that and put it down to maternal instinct, which she supposed was always tinged with fear.

But this fear is different. Some women, she has read, never notice anything. In her experience, one or two are surprisingly slow on the uptake. But Madeleine knows the signs. She doesn't want to feel this understanding, splitting her head like an atom; exposing the dark, dirty inside.

On a shelf in Ben's office—the box room—she finds the book she knew was there. She takes it down and blows dust off the top. The spine is broken, the pages bent. She should put it back. She thumbs through, glancing at the bright photographs and familiar names; remembering trips to out-of-the-way heaths and cliff tops. She had been so delighted by his unlikely interest. On some pages are his scribbled notes. Hearing the excitement in his words makes her cry.

It's a short step from the shelf to his jacket, on the back of the chair. Her stomach twists but she carries on. She hears Clare's voice: 'Just investigate.' She goes through the pockets methodically; then, sure she's missed something, starts again. She searches the desk drawers; looks through his spare briefcase, his papers.

She should know what to look for. But she can find nothing.

She imagines the blackbirds' nest: sturdy and strong, holding a clutch of eggs, which she now knows are blue-green and speckled. She pictures the thin shell, shattering; the soft, damp body unfurling.

When she went into labour he came to the hospital with her. Then she knew she had won.

The afternoon sun slants across the papers on her desk. Madeleine has managed to push through the dull end-of year summary of a charity's good works.

The noise takes her by surprise: the blackbirds are chak-chak-chaking, shrill and loud. It's a few moments before she sees them: one on the patio, the other on the lawn. They are both frantic, squawking.

On the fence, a large bird is perched above the ivy: a young magpie, its slim body agile, head cocked to one side.

Madeleine watches, transfixed. The magpie hops delicately along the wood. The blackbirds run at it, flapping and squawking, and it backs off. But it soon returns.

She is half-out of her chair, leaning into the window.

Before she can move the magpie jumps down, onto the old greenery. It scrabbles against the leaves, its wings wide, searching for the nest. Its awkward flapping and struggling, where before was only grace, is raw desire: revealed and shocking. The blackbirds shriek, helpless on the lawn, on the fence; but they dare come no nearer.

The magpie dips its head.

Madeleine bangs on the window and the intruder flies away, a small shape dangling from its beak. Then it hops under a shrub, pinning its prize to the soil with one claw and pecking at it.

She unlocks the back door and rushes out into the cold wind. The magpie flies off. Under the shrub the chick lies on the soil. Its wings are half-feathered, blue-black; its thin-skinned, bulging belly is bare. She scoops the bird onto her palm, and it waves its claws feebly. Its eyes are closed, and bleeding. Its chest moves softly. She holds the chick, stroking its head. When it is completely still, she replaces it on the soil and goes back into the house, feeling the loss inside her: a small, fluttering heart.

An hour or so later, the blackbirds' shrieking starts up again. Madeleine's stomach lurches. She looks out. The magpie is back, sitting on the fence. She bangs on the window and it flies off.

For the rest of the afternoon, as the garden slips into shadow, she is poised at her desk, ready to strike the glass.

At five o'clock the landline goes. Ben's mobile number shows in the display. Madeleine listens to his message: he has another late meeting; she should eat without him. She tries to picture him in his office at school, but finds she can't. She looks out. The magpie is back.

She watches its relentless advance. It cocks its head towards the window, and in that pitiless eye she sees reflected her own: searching for the weak spot, the way in.

She runs upstairs, and takes the folded blanket from the end of the bed. She hurries back down, and out to the garden shed for a chair, and the broom. She sets the chair a few feet from the blackbirds' nest, but not so near as to scare them. It's cold. The breeze makes the daffodils nod and sway, and blows dead leaves across the grass. She wraps herself in the blanket and grips the broom, waving it whenever the magpie comes near. This works, for a while. But the blackbirds are confused by her presence, and take fright when she hisses at the magpie, so she has to move further back.

And then the intruder seems to sense she is powerless. It hardly bothers to fly away, just lifts its wings and half-runs a few yards. Then it perches, watching, waiting for her to give up.

Soon she sees that another magpie has appeared, on the ridge of next door's roof.

They are working together.

Now Madeleine can't suppress the memory: the scent of cooking; wild flowers in a jar. The gift—the book that revealed how well she knew him—carelessly handed over, under the other's puzzled gaze. Laughing with him, over the inedible meal that was laid out.

The sense of something unstoppable: already begun.

Two small, dark-haired boys, brought in to say goodnight.

Madeleine sits upright in the chair and grips the broom. The magpie watches from the top of the fence.

She can stay out here all night, if she has to.

Martin Willitts, Jr.

We Are Where We Always Were

Vase with Violet Irises against a Yellow Background
Based on the Van Gogh painting, 1890
'I need air, I feel overwhelmed with boredom and grief' — letter to Theo, #631,
1890

I need air. Let the room expand its lungs.
I am restless as leaves in gusts of wind.
Boredom is a gale breaking shutters, and snapping spines of trees.

I begin repairs with enthusiasm,
but the doctors despair of my frequent relapses
dooming me to failure before I can begin.

I shall close myself to their concerns, and open the barred windows!
The citron background and Prussian blue irises are all I need.
And Air! Paintbrushes dabs of air! Illuminated light of air!

My renewal begins, like a vase with colors of air,
like a woman unaware of her breathtaking rapture,
like a man thrashing wheat never tired of cutting air.

Yellow and violet are tremendously disparate complementary,
making love with air, that I cannot stop drawing it into my skin.
No more boredom and grief. Bring me packages of air! Let me sing!

Majolica Jar with Branches of Oleander

Based on the painting by Van Gogh, 1888
'...as free in the open air and as much a flower as anything could be'—Letter
527 about Manet's paintings of peonies

An echo of Japan, a smudge of haiku,
softness of a crane feather—

where is the poetry but in flowers?

The sun rises over mountains, like Koi.
Paper lanterns have calligraphy names of the dead.

Where are the poems of flowers?

Women are shorelines where fishing boats toss nets
to catch oleanders, sparkling with opposite colors.

Where are the flowers singing love poems?

The sun never sets like a crane in the silence,
papery as lanterns of Koi in the smudges of love.

I am a flowering poem finding my way to you.

Aisling Tempany

Unrequited Love

The unrequited love starts from nothing really.
A joke expanded into a thought of 'you and me.'
Turns filler words and pronouns into a great delight
or the cruellest pain.

They are religiously transformed, in words never spoken.
They cease being people: petty and flawed,
and are as infallible objects, piously obeyed.
Like God above, they never reciprocate.

Till some day the irrationality of the dream
becomes an unrequited rejection.
A consuming hatred for a man
with bad teeth and grey hair.

The Rules

The cloaked man reads his words,
Long learnt, and never changing,
made in another time and place.

He talks of a stranger
while hands count beads.
(If you count them wrong,
exactly what happens)
Like workers in a factory, they bend
and stand, and bend and walk.
His monotone mumble is of
ancient words and dead pronouns

with nothing said of here and now
just the rules, repeated always.

Reading the Cards

I The Magician

He is a creative fire, demanding awe.
A manipulating fire!
Meditate on him, and you will create
great works of art
perfectly aligned with the forces of nature
If you don't, you're selfish
and all your dreams will founder.

VI: The Lovers

A gentleman, a lady in a gown.
LOVE. Romance and Compassion
Harmony, and fruitfulness
between two people.
The dignified partnership!
It only exists between man and woman,
between duality, the polarity of energies.
(That's a euphemism surely?)
Man and woman, man and woman.
Brother and sister – that love is fine.
That one is still dignified.
It's the rapport of man and woman.

VIII: The Moon

The person who sees this card
has the kind of rational mind
that doesn't look at tarot cards.
At pictures of Odysseus and Manannan
that explain how the world works to them.
It's a card of high art, and low morals.
It's a card that questions your sexuality.
You, of the rational mind.

The Dead Skipper
Jonathan Carr

Every afternoon, when we climbed up Church Street from the beach, he was sitting out in the garden, a rug over his knees and the sun in his face, staring out to sea. His eyes were a bright pale blue, like dots of sky, and with his wavy white hair and wrinkles he looked as old as God. Nobody knew who he was or where he'd come from.

My Mum and Dad told us to stay away from him, though they never said why. Tim, who thought he knew everything, said it was obvious, wasn't it? The weirdo was a Russian spy. But spies couldn't be that ancient, I said, and if he really was a spy why wasn't he hiding until it got dark, instead of sitting outside like a statue where everyone could see him? Tim went cross-eyed and dropped his shoulders, dangling his arms like a spastic. Dah! It's a double bluff, thicko! I didn't know what a double bluff was, so I called out 'liar' and headbutted him. My Dad had to separate us.

There were railings at the end of the old man's front garden, the same as with every other house on the street. But nobody else had a rusty anchor on the far side, so big it must have come off one of the tankers that crossed the bay. Not that it was a real anchor any more, because there were no ropes or chains and it wasn't holding anything down. But if I climbed onto the wall, sucked in my breath and hung over the spikes, I could touch it. I told myself touching it would bring me good luck.

I started doing that every day on the way home. He never saw me because he was too busy watching the sea, even when there wasn't a boat in sight. Sometimes he looked at the sky too. It was odd that he always sat in the chair in exactly the same way, never moving. I tried to see whether he was still breathing, but I couldn't really tell. Perhaps he was dead and wanted to be put out in the sun each day rather than get cold underground. If you had to be dead, it seemed a better way to do it. And sometimes it looked like the light hung round his head, the same as you saw in churches. I decided to call him the Dead Skipper because if he wasn't yet, he would be soon.

One morning, we were told never to look at the sun. Do it just once, and we'd never be able to see anything ever again. Why only today? I wanted to know. My Dad told us the sun was always dangerous, but that today it was really really dangerous. Don't dare look at it! Then he said something about the moon getting in its way. You mean they're going to hit each other? I asked. No, they'll go past each other, like ships at sea. But, I said, if they're only going past each other...

Tim started to do his impression of a scratchy record getting stuck. He never liked it when I was the one who asked questions.

There was a moment, Dad said, when you could only see the one that was nearest. It didn't sound right to me, because I knew the moon was nearer than the sun, and the moon wasn't even there during the day. If we do look, I wanted to know, will it be like dying? Worse, my Dad replied. Don't you even think about it. But why will it be worse? I always thought dying was the worstest worst.

Tim made the record sound again, squeakier this time. That did it. I pushed him over, sat on him, grabbed his hair and pulled. The squeak soon turned into a squeal. Tim may be older than me, and cleverer, but I'm bigger.

My Dad told us to stop it. That's enough, both of you. Make up.

We had to make up, the same as we always did. I'm sorry, said Tim. I'm sorry, I agreed. We weren't sorry, neither of us. It was just one of those things we had to say to keep the grown-ups happy.

On account of the moon getting in the way of the sun, we came home very early from the beach that day, when it was still morning. I'd taken some quick looks at the sky, but that was all. Of course, the sun was there, the same as always. I could feel it. And the sea was silvery as the bathroom mirror.

As we climbed up Church Street, Tim and I were a long way behind my Dad. We were wearing yellow life-jackets and carrying an oar each. I was half-holding, half-dragging mine. It was steep, especially at the corner where the Dead Skipper lived, though it wasn't really a corner, more of a slow curve. He was in his chair as usual, staring into the sun. That meant, if he wasn't already dead, he was about to be worse than dead. It was my last chance. For days, I had been daring myself to hop over the fence, prod him with the oar and run away, fast as I could, up the hill and out of sight. If he didn't do anything, I'd know he really was dead and not just pretending.

When we got near the railings, I stopped Tim and whispered in his ear.

He said it was a silly idea.

I dared him.

He tried to keep pretending it was silly, but I'd dared him so I knew he'd have to do it in the end.

The iron railings, with their pointy tops, looked much bigger than I'd thought they were. Leaning over them was one thing. Jumping was something else. I thought about trying the gate. It would scrape and creak and, if there was even the littlest bit of life still in him, he'd be bound to notice. Anyway, it looked stuck.

I wasn't going to say anything, but my legs had gone all gooey. And my tummy felt as though it was trying to giggle. I balanced the oar against the railings, but didn't look at Tim as I led the countdown. Three, two, one.

We both climbed up onto the wall at the same time. I don't think I really decided to do it, or not to do it. I just heard my shorts rip as I scrambled over the railings, and wondered how I would explain that to Mum. Grabbing the oar, I stood still. And then I heard a noise coming out of me. It took a moment to realise it was my own breath, flapping like a loose sail in the wind.

Dead or about to be worse-than-dead, he must surely have noticed us by now. But if he had, he wasn't letting on. He didn't even turn his head our way.

We were standing in a flower bed, but it didn't look as though there had been any flowers there for a long time. I rubbed the end of the anchor for a lot of luck. The oar in my hands was pointing up at Heaven. The life-jacket burped whenever I moved, so I didn't. Tim was still too, except for his hands, which I could see had got the shakes. Typical.

The Dead Skipper looked much bigger, this close up, even though he was only sitting down. What if he stood up? I hadn't thought of that. The idea of him moving at all was scary.

He was dressed the same as usual, like he'd just come out of the sea, with waders up to his thighs, baggy dark blue trousers and a woolly sweater. On top, he was white everywhere, his head and face all sprayey with hair, and his hands looked like two hairy knots mooring him to the arms of the chair.

And when I looked at the house, I had a shock. It had always seemed ordinary enough from the street, but I must've never looked properly before.

Some of the windows weren't real windows at all. They had boards in them, blocking out the light. They made the house seem spooky.

Only now did I remember the oars and what we were meant to do with them. I wasn't sure it was a good idea any more, but one push and we would know. I turned to Tim and counted under my breath. He still wouldn't look at me. He was staring at the Dead Skipper. It was so hard to whisper, I was afraid I might start coughing. Three, two, one.

I was about to do it. I really was.

But the Dead Skipper began to speak. He wasn't actually looking at us, but his lips were moving. And his voice, though it rumbled like the bottom notes of the organ on Sundays, didn't seem unfriendly. There wasn't a Russian accent, as far as I could tell.

What were we carrying uphill today? he asked.

I heard the question okay, and there was nothing mad about it, but I didn't have time to say anything back before things went wrong. At first, I thought Tim was going to bash him on the top of the head with his oar. Either that, or he was losing his grip on it, because it was whirling through the air. Then I realised it only looked like that because he was turning round to jump back over the railings. Next thing, there was this clattering sound and a car going up the street blew its horn. The oar was lying in the street. Tim's voice had gone squeaky and he was mixing his words up, saying things like I had to come with him or else, that he would tell on me, that spies killed people, that I was going to die. Stuff like that.

Of course I was scared, but I wasn't that scared.

The Dead Skipper looked to be smiling, though it was hard to tell. His mouth was crusted with beard like a barnacle.

Oh dear, he said in that booming voice, I seem to have scared off your friend.

He's my brother, I explained. My elder brother, even though he's smaller than me. And about your question, I said, I'm carrying a life-jacket uphill, though I'm not really carrying it because I'm wearing it. And an oar.

A life-jacket? An oar?

It seemed he didn't like my answer. I could feel myself going red, and I thought about running away after Tim before he could get out of his chair and... Blimey! Now I understood. That's why

66

the anchor was there, in the garden. He was going to tie me up to it.

We sail too, I added, making for the railings as fast as I could.

But the oar got stuck or I dropped it or something. And I tripped.

Are you hurt?

No, sir, I said in a voice gone all scaredy-cat.

Come here.

I stayed where I was.

You sail?

Yes sir. 'Sail' seemed to be okay, from the way he said it. We sail *miles and miles!* That went down better still.

Where's your ship?

Pulled up on the beach, I said.

Where are you going?

Nowhere special.

I didn't like him asking me where I was going, because he would know how to catch me. But then I changed my mind because though he obviously wasn't dead, he didn't look as though he was going to murder me either.

So I told him the truth, that I was a skipper the same as he was and that one day I was going to sail my ship across the whole world, all the way to the end.

What's your name?

Captain Hurricane. He's in *Valiant*.

I noticed he was smiling, and the sun was shining so bright on his eyes I wondered if they might catch fire.

He said everyone dreamed of sailing to the end of the world but that most people were too scared to do it. I told him I wasn't scared, not a bit. And some of them leave it too late, he said, and by then they've lost their nerve. So start early, he told me. I promised him I would.

Then I asked him why he wanted to be worse than dead. I told him everyone knew that if you looked at the sun today, it would be worse than death. The moon was going to get in its way.

This didn't sound any righter than when Dad said it. But I was proud to be able to tell him.

Is that so? he said.

I nodded my head a few times, but he still didn't look at me. I realised that he had never looked at me, all the time I had been there, which was ages.

He asked me whether I trusted him. I told him I might.

I'm going to turn off the sun, he said, just for a while. I told him nobody could do that. Only God.

I want you to look at me, he said, not the sun.

That was when I heard my Dad calling from somewhere. Tim must've told him where I was.

Please hurry up, I said. I've got to go.

He did hurry up.

Look at me, he said again. And don't look at the sun.

No sir.

Promise?

Cross my heart, sir, and hope to die.

The next moment the whole world went dark and cool, except only for his blue eyes. They were huge and terribly bright, like they'd taken all the light out of the world. I couldn't stop staring at them. I just couldn't.

My Dad was still calling. But maybe Tim hadn't sneaked on me, because he sounded further away than before.

And anyway I couldn't go because I'd made a promise.

It seemed to stay like that for ever and ever.

The Dead Skipper was there the next day as usual, staring at the sea.

I never told anyone what He had done.

Eluned Rees

His Beauty is all External

She spends the day
counting falling seed-heads,
thinking about his bull-finch sun —
as yellow-red
as a grain of lunar magma.

He curls round her
like a mollusc shell
all winter, spring;
staring through the dark
at the squared-off panes of glass —
at the reflection
of his bruise-prints
on her tender skin.

If she leaves him again,
he will kill.

Tomorrow she'll wake new
for a single day, or a season —
like other, primitive kinds
which change identities;

she'll wake from the slumber
of her nymph years —
arms flailing; abseiling
into the air-borne blue
of soft bodied may-flies.

The Paradise of Los Leonnes

Zaida, Zoraida and Zorahaida
spill wine over our necks,
eat saffron cakes preserved with spices
hauled over the phosphate mountain.

They talk of Marraquesh;
of apple-mint tea
and the stink of goat hides
drying on the roof tops;
of the journey North
through the mists of the Rif,
and the hand-painted tiles
in the palaces of Grenada.

The sisters tip basin after basin of water
over pebbles in the rills; watch the diamond-cut
reflection of a feather trail: a trembling flight
across the poplar groves of Las Amedas,

Beneath the locked stairwells
of the Alhambra,
snow melt from the Massif
descends the Sierra Nevada,
spouts up the grey-green veins
of a lemon tree,
flushes out a fox-hole—

filling the crumbling arteries
of the fort, with creamy salts
to plump the onions,
shine the peppers.

Beneath key-hole arches
the bitter scent of crushed juniper
is held in the breath of women's days.

Red dust blooms in the air
over the heads of boys
kicking a football in the clay hills;
we, the stone lions,
guard the Caliph's daughters.

Jane McLaughlin

Going to Gullfoss

Black crags on the skyline.
Even in August
this wind cuts sharp.

The heath
where blueberry and holy grass
line the paths.

The only signs
a white smoke rising.
A far voice of water.

To the edge. And then only
the terraces of the canyon
under the white deluge roaring down.

Gullfoss:
the water that falls
gold in sunshine.

In grey as now,
white over the tumbling steps,
a race of white horses.

The falls
throw the air upwards
with a hand of thunder.

Every glacial stream
winding this dark plain
every pond and lake

feed the Hvita river
cascading now
bigger and more violent than love.

Mudslide

The air moved like silk, like silk
her silk dress rippled
past the olive trees.
Under a cinnamon sky
she gathered fruit
  winter-fed with rain.

Mars sat like a red plum
over the sea mist
  and the hillside moved.

The road is fractured still
none of the lights working.
Winter still moves like water, like water
  under the hot powder of the beanfield.

Some died in their cars
under earth and trees
as the mud slipped like silk, like water.
Upended roots bake in midsummer;
the hillside houses clasp their cracked footings,
  bleeding geraniums from their eyes.

The coast trains begin to crawl
down the shaken lines
past the bright fruit of the beaches.
The water over hair and skin
weaving a dress of rippled silk
leaving the slopes dried to a craze
  the lights dumb as clay.

After the Reading

It is pelting frozen snow.
The poets fan out into the night
wearing a variety of hats.

Coldest October night for decades.
My best pashmina
sogs to a sop in the blizzard.

The street is empty except for
snow spiralling in gusts.
The awning of the chic café is refuge.
How warm they look inside.

No traffic, especially not taxis.

I pull my wet shawl off my hair,
remember it's Diwali, that somewhere
you'll be dancing.

At last the eye of a yellow light:
I shut the door on the teeming flakes.

On the seat is a new novel
just signed by the author.

There will be fireworks in the snow.

It's been two years, and I have no lamps to light.

Beachy Head

if they left scars
or grazes of blood
down the bleached chalk
if the sea prowling at the foot
of the headlong cliff
did not swallow its prey quietly
without a trace
they might be able to count
to know how many
are the lost and nameless
who take that last step
over the falling edge
and dive like hawks
after the prey of escape

Ron Carey

Among Men

There are a few originals left—a small curmudgeon
Of diehards, one might say. Life has put something
Sharp in our water or something shaky beneath
Our pale, Tupperware skin. We're not complaining.
That's just the way of it. No hand-holding, Thank
God but we are interested in each other, the way old
Walruses might care who has slipped from the rocks
And not returned to shore. By day we live below
The buzz of halogen—daylight been removed. Later,
Staff Nurse clops in with a fairytale of rain and night.
At lights, some new man might let the side down. But
We are careful not to hear. By breakfast clash, we have
Regained our manliness—ready now to face the dead
Certainty of priests; prognosing doctors and the knife.

Catching My Death

At the edge of March,
Morning is waiting
For the chilled sun to come
Between
The hawthorns,
Dazzling.
I find life now—much the same
As the robin does—wriggling
In my mouth.

By evening, in my garden
Pomp, when
The ground has removed
Its stiff, white coat,
To pierce
Its frozen heart,
I make my first incision
Beneath
Its knotted ribs.

Cathy says, one day
I'll catch my death
On Watergrasshill
And lie, un-found, spilt
As sunshine,
Until
The Earth warms
And the soil opens
To the resurrection of the worms.

Ride a Cock Horse

Behind the bars of *Adam's Used Car Sales*, he found
Margaret's killer; fierce, black and powerful, waiting
To be sold. He knew the licence; its numbers and letters
Had rung little bells of death in the hushed Courtroom.
He had to sell some of Margaret's best things to buy it.
Weeks later, the Jaguar still sat on the gravel; watching
The silver Micras feed at the Avenue's green edge.

He had imagined taking it into the Wicklow Mountains,
To their secret, *Glean Na Smol*. And burning it to death.
Its flames would reach high; scorching the glittering feet
Of stars they had named together. By its consoling heat,
Drunk perhaps, he would cry himself out. Then, even in
Heavy rain, he would walk all the way home and leave
Its smoking carcass; a dramatic sacrifice to her memory.

But, on the day he drove it home, he was surprised how well
The wheels sucked the road; how the car wrapped round
And hugged him close. The luxury of soft leather; the clarity
Of the sound system; the easy pleasure of the turning wheel.
He had driven it, hard, every day. Each morning he woke
Feeling a little guilty. Would Margaret understand? Yes.
Well, maybe. She never knew much about cars anyway.

In the House of Lazarus

He wakes to find the journey
Still in his bones.
Outside, in dust-filled trees
A golden oriole sings;
Its song grows stronger
With the rising heat.
He swings his legs out.
A rivulet of blood
Has dried between his toes.
His sandals lie tattered
Against the wall, taking
The scent of limestone.

In the courtyard round
Water rises, like the sound
Of a crowd.
In the courtyard a woman
Prepares the grain.
On the saddle quern
The stone rolls away.
He washes himself and takes
Pleasure in being clean.
In the mirror, he sees how
Thin he has become.
And in his long black hair
The first strand of grey.

Blind Faith
Michelle Shine

1 Samuel 16

Samuel Anoints David

2. Samuel said, 'How can I go? If Saul hears about this he will kill me.'
The LORD said, 'Take a heifer with you and say, "I have come to sacrifice
to the LORD"

My husband comes from far away, so I've only seen him once
before. It was the afternoon he came to speak to my father. My
mother said I wasn't allowed anywhere near the room. But I am
curious by nature and sat down on the sill of the casement
opposite the slightly open door. I leaned back against the window
and the sun warmed my back. Then feeling invulnerable I edged
closer, leaned down and wedged behind the door, closing one eye
and watching the proceedings through a crack. He didn't catch
even one glimpse of me. His eyes never strayed in my direction,
not once. Not once, but I saw him perfectly.

They were in the drawing room. He, Mr Lavinsky, was in the
wing chair in front of the bookcase where daddy keeps his
Hebrew texts. My father sat opposite and I could only see the
back of his head.

'So the women have done their deal and you are pleased with
the dowry,' my father said.

'I have seen a picture of your daughter and I am very pleased,
yes.'

'I have an elder daughter too, who is perhaps,' my father
paused. I imagined him showing Mr Lavinsky his open palms.
'More interesting,' he finally said.

'The one I have seen already is incredibly beautiful. I think I'm
in love.'

'Love,' my father said, walking over to Mr Lavinsky and
handing him a picture. No doubt one made by my artist brother
in charcoal on parchment, probably, a likeness of me.

My father is not a typical rabbi. He says he's a theologian not a
fundamentalist. He could be mistaken for a shopkeeper. Only on

special occasions does he wear black. Grey trousers are usual, and he's often without a jacket so his waistcoat is exposed. All his shirts are collarless. He does, of course, wear a *kippa*.

'Love is something you grow into because your wife is lovely... inside.' My father stabbed his two hands into his belly, as if struck by an arrow. Then stood aside so I could once again see Mr Lavinsky. Ginda. I think it is appropriate that I should call him Ginda, with his thick hair the colour of chestnuts, and irises to match fearlessly seeking out my father.

'You are an orphan.'

Ginda's lips, fleshy, pink, and flecked with white skin, no doubt from biting winds. I shut my eyes, tried to imagine his naked body up against mine. I could almost feel the rough skin around his mouth.

'Yes, I am,' Ginda said.

'Certainly, otherwise you would not have come here alone.'

'I work hard. I will cherish and take care of your daughter.'

'I understand that you are not a butcher, baker, or holy man. These are troubled times. I wouldn't be surprised if the only way to make a living in the future would be to provide sustenance for the community, and maybe clothes and shoes.'

My father wandered over to the window. I had to lean to one side to see him bunch the embroidered curtain in one hand. He looked out over the golden hay fields newly harvested by the farmers in his congregation. My father's wire framed glasses caught a ray and glinted. He purposefully turned towards Ginda and asked, 'What is it that you do, again?'

'I own a horse and cart.'

'So you ferry things?'

'Yes, sir.'

'People, their possessions, that sort of thing.'

'Yes, sir.'

'When people are short of money they carry things and walk.'

'Yes sir, but I'm constantly busy.'

'How come?'

'You forget the elderly cannot walk. And I'll take any passenger. I'm rarely given coins, but everyone in my town has been good to me. I have food, I have clothes, I have friends, I even have a home. And the few coins that came my way I saved to buy a second horse and cart. It's already agreed; I will rent it out to a farmer for a small weekly fee.'

81

My father paced.

'To marry a rabbi's daughter is a *mitzvah*, you know that?'

I want to rush in and say, 'Daddy, please, he is a good man, don't give him such a hard time.'

My mother squeezed through the kitchen door. I heard the rustle of her clothes and looked up. She would have shooed me away, but she was carrying glasses of tea, a small bowl of sugar, and a plate of homemade biscuits on a tray. Her stern eyes met mine conveying everything and nothing at all. As she entered the drawing room the door groaned. Her shoes squeaked every time she put her left foot forward into the room.

'Do you want me to bring in Hannah?' she asked my father, offering him the tray. He twirled his finger in the sugar bowl digging up a particularly lumpy piece of cane. He placed it in his mouth, took a glass from the tray and noisily sucked the hot steaming liquid through the sweetness.

'Offer our guest, go on,' he said to her.

For a second or two she seemed to be in some sort of trance. Then she nodded and like a serving wench, bent her knees as she offered Ginda his tea.

'Thank you, Mrs Aizenburg, thank you, so much.'

'You are welcome,' my mother said, as he took his glass.

I squirmed.

My father was lost to the bales on the horizon.

'Ginda Lavinsky, you will want to see her,' my mother said. 'I will go and fetch her in.'

There was no table in the room, so she left the tray on the floor and flurried past me. When she returned she was ceremoniously linking arms with my sister who bowed her head. It was as if my sister was the bride. She is small with wild red hair and luminous green eyes. She has a way of tilting her face to the side and half smiling that makes you feel she is taking you into her confidence. She doesn't realise she's doing it.

'It's nerves, Hannah,' she once said to me.

'Nerves?' I wanted to shout at her then from my position in the hall. 'Then why as soon as you are in the room is it suddenly transformed? The hairline cracks in the vase over there seem like art. The painting of the *chazzan* speaks of music. Ginda is entranced. There are reasons, Esther, but they are not nerves.'

Instead, I watched as she sat on the footstool that was kicked aside from our father's chair. Our parents stood at opposite ends of the room. She was in the middle looking from one to the other. Neither of them returned her gaze. She twirled her hair.

'Hello,' she said to Ginda, looking at him at last with her fiery green eyes.

'Hello Hannah.' His words blew away from him, rising like soap bubbles. 'Do you think you will be happy to marry me?'

I swallowed hard.

She looked towards our father. His attention was once again back in the room, although not on the scene that was playing out before him, but at the watch he pulled out of his pocket by its chain. Then Esther twisted her body toward our mother who, like a scarecrow, stared ahead.

'Yes,' Esther said to Ginda, but the word caught in her throat, so she said it again. 'Yes.'

'I will be a very good husband. I will see to all your needs.'

Esther nodded, twirling her hair frantically. She lowered her eyes to the carpet that my father bought my mother last year for *Chanukah*, so that guests will no longer see the cracks in the floor.

'Yes,' Esther said again, her voice tremulous, whispering.

I wanted to run in, grab Ginda's arm and say, 'I will love and treasure you, have your children and keep your home. I might be old and not beautiful, as my sister is, but I am passionate. I read books. I have thoughts. You will be able to discuss worldly affairs and all your problems with me. I will understand things in a way that Esther could never do.'

'Is there anything else that the two of you would like to say to each other?' our father asked.

Esther shook her head.

'Yes, I would like to ask you sir, when there are others more eligible who live closer, why has your family chosen me for Hannah?'

'Why? Because *shidduchs* are made at birth but my husband did not think that was necessary,' my mother said, coming swiftly alive, sweeping the unsweetened tea out of Ginda's hands, and placing it on the tray with a clatter. Moving across the room to hold her husband's gaze and relieve him also of the burden of an empty glass.

Perhaps Ginda became aware of my presence then, as slave to my ego's fragility, I sped through the narrow hallway to the bedroom that Esther and I shared. And if he didn't hear my loud footsteps, then surely he would have heard me slam the door at least. I so wanted him to. Throwing myself down on the mattress I sobbed until my face stung and my head ached and throbbed. I hate self-pity, it is an ugly emotion. But what I felt was pure self-pity and it seemed to justify my ugliness. It was all going to go horribly wrong. How could it not? Like a rotten fruit I lay discarded, contaminated and bad.

The bed is stripped bare. The linen washed and folded at the bottom of the trunk. My mother kneels before me. She has pins in her mouth even though all the alterations have already been made. I stand on a box. I'm wearing a white satin bridal gown, bluish with age. My mother irons it with her hands.

'You are taller and a little skinnier than I was when I wore this. But look at you.' We both look in the mirror set in the wardrobe door. I look like an arum lily. My reflection is speckled with rusty dots on the glass. I never noticed them before. They seem ominous.

Esther is out in the yard singing the wedding march with Isaac, the baby of our family. Their joyful notes reach me through the open window. She is laughing, gleefully, pleased that she will not be leaving home today.

I am nervous, more so than any other ordinary bride. I haven't slept or eaten for weeks. My husband-to-be thinks I'm someone else who has answered to my name. She is naturally graceful. I am gangly with mousey hair. Her facial features are soft. Mine are over-large and shocking. Her skin is smooth. My left cheek is discoloured, rough and inflamed. She is rainbowesque and full of promise. I am intense and pale.

My day is threatening rain. I am not surprised. In the distance music wavers in the blowy air. The men must be leaving their homes linking arms and dancing with bottles balanced on their heads. The ululating women must be shaking their breasts behind a tall divide.

My mother stands up, holding onto my dress for stability. I nearly topple. She takes the veil that is hanging down behind me and draws it slowly down over my face.

'It will be fine,' she says. "You'll see.'

I can't see.

I can't see her eyes.

I can't see anything.

All week there have been feasts. To celebrate my demons

84

washed away in a flowing stream. To celebrate my husband's deepening alignment to God. Tonight, the whole town is invited to the party in the square. If there is a cloudburst and it is cold then there is the risk of influenza and all the guests will be given food to eat in their homes.

I am walking through the rubble street on my mother's arm. My veil guards my identity and blinds me. My legs are trembling. My heart thumps wildly in my chest.

'Hannahla,' my grandma calls.

I raise my arm a little to show that I can hear her. The ground is slippery and sticky with mud. I hold my dress a few inches above the earth. No one stops me. Today my ankles are considered less private than my face.

When we arrive in the square I lift my veil slightly to look beneath. My mother slaps my wrist. Faint drops of rain wet my arms. Everything is where it is supposed to be. The congregation are all seated, women behind the men peeping through a velvet curtain. And to the side of them, the aisle that leads to the *chuppah*. Four poles, wound with lilies and ivy, hold up the canopy. Ginda stands under it with his back to me, my father before him, wearing his clerical robes. The voices of the choir are beseeching my fertility. I make a low deep sound in my throat. A hand appears under my veil holding a silver cup. The scent of its content is potent and sharp. My mother's hand shakes. There is a wave in the cup that threatens to make a red stain reach my dress. My heart turns as she says, 'Go on mamala, drink.'

I take a sip but it does not numb me like wine is supposed to do. The cup disappears too soon. My mother holds my arm. Someone else holds my other arm. I am aware of a hundred stares in my direction as we walk slowly down the aisle, and up steps to the raised platform under the *chuppah*. My mother makes sure I do not trip over my dress.

I have arrived. She places me next to Ginda. I can smell lemon mixed with manly perspiration. I can hear the racing of his breath. He leans towards me. His voice is husky and full of longing as he whispers, 'Hello.'

I am afraid to answer him. My mouth is drier than desert sands. The wind flaps the canopy above us. A spray of rain showers my hands. My teeth don't stop chattering. It's not cold. *This*, Esther, is nerves.

Overhead, a flock of crows cry. My father begins his chant. I feel so weak it is a wonder I do not faint. Then Ginda's arm sweeps against my own. I shiver from the feel of him. My mother holds my veil and wine is offered to me again. I am too intent on Ginda's brown wrist, the hairs by his white cuff and a hint of yeast. The cup retreats before it reaches my lips.

Ginda answers my father's questions in Hebrew. His voice is too keen. Next, my mother is leading me to circle my groom seven times. When I come to stand beside the man again he pledges his vows to me. I hear shuffling and fidgeting from immediately behind.

'Huh!' it is my intake of breath, and even though I can't see, I turn to ascertain what the problem might be. It is solved. Ginda places a hand gently on my arm, slides a ring up to the index knuckle of my right hand. I close my eyes knowing that the moment has come. He lifts my veil. I lift my lids to look pleadingly into his eyes. He steps backwards away from me.

'No,' he says, shaking his head.

They have their arms around his shoulders. Those men. The ushers. My father's friends. They are holding him up.

'She's a rabbi's daughter.' The words come from his left.

'Ginda, don't think you can do better,' says the man on his right.

My father places himself once again before him, 'This is my gift to you. She is lovely… inside.'

I watch as the tears well in my husband's chestnut eyes. Someone places a glass at his feet.

'Ginda,' my mother whispers, 'You must break the glass.'

Ginda is held like a prisoner searching for a friendly face. I wish they would let go of him. In spite of myself, I wish he could run.

I stand alone and ashamed.

'Ginda,' my father says. 'You must honour your pledge.'

To the left of me, the fiddler waits with his bow poised above the strings.

Ginda is pushed. He smashes the glass with his foot and screams, 'No!' The word flies away as the crowd yells, '*Mazel-tov!*'

Jean Atkin

Janet Hunter Remembers Her Man

He said, you had to be there
in the heart-thump and stars
and see the whales rise up

black and blowing through
the herring. When the sea split
with silver and

the air leapt with water
all the glitter and livewire
of herring.

You had to be there, he said,
watching water roll
like mercury

from cautious oars, the men
whispering to the gill nets
in the bows.

He said, it was the moon,
the herring love
the moon

The Finned Man of Rascarrel

He claimed his father heard it
from his wife's father, the tale
of the day the finned man
beached himself
on the shore at Rascarrel.

At neap tide each May he liked to tell
how a child came shrieking
to the haaf nets to fetch the men;
and the way they took a shovel,
new sharpened just that morning.

How they went, and stood around him
in a circle, taking in
his colour, and the way the skinny
dorsal down his back
rose and fell
with his breathing.

How when they asked his name
and business, he made
some sound they took to be
a hunting cry of whales;
But they knew his cursing solid

as the splay of limpets;
and when he shouted
they said his salt tongue broke
on the rocks
and fell back hissing
through the shingle.

They put the shovel by.
And then they rolled him
over and over
wading together
into deep water.

Murmuration

The starlings lean
like woodsmoke on the fields,
and blow away.

Bedded in leaves the Wood of Cree
aches in the gale
and sleepwalks into winter.

Rain maps the hills.
Our roaming thoughts
drain down to silt.

Your house is filled with hollow coats.
The mice climb in the walls,
familiar ghosts.

The starlings start to tilt,
they make an end, pull out their stitches,
fold, descend.

David Olsen

After First Frost

You lean on a rake and chat
while a neighbour clears gutters
and downspouts of blackened leaves
that fall again like unreformed
miscreants. New England's hard
on a weathered clapboard house,
and something always needs doing:
windowsills and eaves exfoliate,
accusing with silent reproach,
and there are galaxies of leaves.

They first began to fall in August
from the weakest cottonwood,
but now aspens and maples moult,
engulfing lawns in piles too deep
for a mulching mower to cope.
You can't allow the leaves
to overwinter in place
because they'd kill the grass,
so you rake a patch and mow
before it's overwhelmed again.

At this rate you only clear
the seventh part of a weekly task;
each day you must do something,
while being grateful for the more
considerate pines. Despite complaints,
you're open to the faltering sun
and avoid flurries of thoughts
of the taut season when closed
neighbours crank reluctant motors
and drive with tense jaws into the sleet.

Vertigo

Once,
I could venture onto a roof
to replace a broken tile,
clear a downspout of fallen leaves,
or align a skewed antenna;
I could balance and bear the risk.

I could go to the edge with you,
trusting the truth of your belay,
where precipice allowed no return
and we held nothing back.
Once upon a fairy-tale time,
I had no fear of falling.

The Moon on a String of Pearls
Nicola Warwick

Midnight and Jacey still isn't home. I untangle my legs from my sheets and creep out onto the landing where the light from my parents' room is escaping under the door. My feet narrowly miss the creaky floorboard. I've memorised where it is so that I won't disturb them, on any of the rare occasions where I might be wandering around at night. I can picture the scene in their room; him lying on his back, snoring, her trying to read, something like a misery memoir or the latest Jodie Picoult, stuck on the same page and worrying about Jacey. I tried one of those books once. It was about two sisters, one's ill, the other is being pressurised into donating a kidney to cure her. Would I do that for Jacey? Would she do it for me?

The door to her bedroom is slightly open, like an invitation. I'm having trouble sleeping tonight, not because I'm worried about her. It's just so hot and I've got a pain in my gut that won't go. Mum's given me an aspirin, but it hasn't helped. I'm restless and can only ease the ache by prowling like a wolf. I've just watched a programme about them and I know that if I could I'd come back as one. They're just like dogs, really, they even wag their tails, which means they're pleased to see you, at least, that's what I think it means. It might be a different story if one was coming towards you and your name was Red Riding Hood.

Jacey's bed hasn't been made properly. She's thrown the duvet over it, but it isn't straight and the pillow still has that flat bit in the middle where her head was last night. The flooring is cold under my feet, but not enough to cool me down. I don't think anything will tonight. Like a dog, I start to sniff at the air in her room. My keen sense of smell tells me it is a mixture of hairspray and perfume, but which one I can't tell. Probably one of the celebrity ones, Kylie or J-LO—she likes that sort of thing. She's left items of make-up on the bed, mascara, eye shadow, lip gloss —I want to try some, but I stop myself because Mum's magazine had an article about germs on make-up brushes and I don't want to catch anything, especially as she's been sleeping with Dave. How do I know that? It's quite easy; even I can work this one out. The week before last, Dave was cleaning his car in our drive. He does it here because he lives in a terraced house with no driveway and he doesn't like to do it in the street. The cars park too close together, he says, to let him clean it properly.

He let me sit inside while he chucked buckets of water over it to rinse away the soap suds. I kept the windows shut. When he wasn't looking, I had a snout in the glove compartment. There was a packet of Durex, right at the front. He hadn't even hidden them, although he could have. There were a packet of tissues and some Trebor mints, too. I put them back pretty quick, but had my evidence. I wasn't surprised as she'd been wearing a halter-neck top a lot of the time and it was obvious she wasn't wearing a bra, although she should have been. She's pretty big in that department and they were quivering about like a couple of blancmanges. That sort of thing would make any man want to sleep with you. I'll remember that for when I'm older. Right now, I'm having trouble convincing Mum I don't need to wear a vest any more. I'm fed up with being the baby.

Sitting on Jacey's bed, I'm not sure what to do now that I've got here. I should have made a plan, really, for moments like this. I'm normally only allowed in when she's here—I have permission to sit on the edge of the bed and watch her do things, like pluck her eyebrows or straighten her hair, things she does for Dave's benefit. He appreciates it because he's sleeping with her. No idea where, though, because he lives with his mum and Jacey lives with us, but I'm sure they've found somewhere to do it.

I look around her room. I know what I'm looking for. Jacey turned eighteen last weekend and Mum and Dad bought her a necklace of pearls. She'd seen someone wearing one in a movie and thought it looked good. And it did. Everyone gathered round and it was 'Don't they suit your skin, Jacey', 'Don't they suit your hair, Jacey'. Auntie June said she looked really glamorous. Nan dabbed her eyes and said she looked just like Mum. Jacey didn't seem too impressed with that. And when I asked if I could try them on, or at least just have a look, she wouldn't let me, said they'd be awful with my lank, mousy hair and nasty, freckly skin. So I didn't even get to see them properly, but now she's not here, I'm going to have a good look.

She has one of those musical jewellery boxes with a ballerina that spins when you open it, but I know it's broken because she hates the tune. The ballerina was last seen lying on her back under a pair of hoop earrings that hang so low when Jacey's wearing them that they nearly reach down to her shoulders. Her hair sometimes catches in them and it just looks daft. The pearls have got to be in there; there's nowhere else they can be. I lift the lid carefully in case that ballerina has been magically mended and is acting like a burglar alarm, but she is lying on her side, next to a diamante brooch from Claire's Accessories, looking like Jacey did after the bottle of sherry she knocked back the first time Mum and Dad left us on our own for a weekend.

The pearls *are* there, coiled round on themselves like a gleaming white snake and in the dark they look like they're glowing. It's too dark to see properly, so I yank one of the curtains open and the moon is out there, full and round, like the mother of all pearls. They'd look great out in the moonlight. There could be some magic to transform me from Cinderella-Little-Sister to fairytale princess, but I'm not going to risk it. Knowing my luck, I'd get out there and be dancing starkers round the front lawn, in the moonlight just as Dave is bringing Jacey home. But I do want to put them on, to feel them against my skin. I reckon they'll be cold. There's a poem by that woman Poet Laureate. We did it at school. It's about a maid is warming the pearls before her mistress puts them on. She does it because she's secretly in love with her. I'm not sure about that, I just think they'd be great against my skin. I'm certain they'll fit better, too, because I'm thinner than Jacey, so they'll hang further down and won't find any obstruction from my flat chest.

They rattle like the bones and teeth of an old skeleton as I shake them out. Now I'm thinking about cannibals from one of those documentaries on Channel 5 Dad likes to watch. I shudder and try not to think of dark-skinned people sucking the marrow from the old bones of explorers. I have to put that idea to one side. It's mad and too creepy to think about. Still, something stops me putting the pearls on. They won't fit over my head; they're not as long as I thought they were. I'd expected them to drape over me and make me look elegant, but there is a little bit of a twist or knot in them that I need to sort out first. So I have to do it properly, unfasten and fasten the catch around my neck, feel them slide over my collar bones and down my pancake chest. But my nails aren't long enough and no matter how hard I pick at the fastener, it won't open. My hands shake as I grip the pearls so tightly that the beads dig into my palms, leaving little round imprints.

The air in the room is hot and still. I feel big and sweaty, as if my hands have been replaced by clumsy paws. My face is filmed with grease. I'm turning into a slimeball. I tug at the string and something I should have known would happen, does. The string breaks snaps and the pearls go bouncing along the floor in a cascade of tiny moons. They sound like hailstones on the conservatory roof. I hold my breath until they stop their movement, the odd one rolling across the floor, its progress becoming louder and louder. The whole street must have heard it. I hold my breath. My heart is bumping against my ribs. Each tiny movement seems to shatter the silence. Luckily, there is no sound from my parents' room.

Kneeling, I try to gather them up, but they have magically become slippery and my fingers struggle as if each bead were wet. My hands are as delicate as shovels. My efforts only encourage them to huddle under the bed and just as I'm ready to crawl under it to tempt them out, a car pulls up outside. It has to be Dave with Jacey. There are a few minutes before she comes in, while they have a kiss and a snog or worse in the car. I know I'll be fine if she doesn't look under the bed. I'll sneak back in after she's gone to work tomorrow. It's a school holiday, so I'll have all day to pick them up and find something to restring them on. Mum will have something in her sewing box. I tip-toe back to my room, crawl in to bed and just lay there, waiting for her to come in.

Somehow, I doze off while I'm waiting, although it's so hot that I'm sweating and sweating so much I'm sure I'm starting to stink like fried onions at the fair. I am a wild animal trapped in its lair, with the hunter waiting outside. I don't know how I manage to sleep as my mind has gone into overdrive, imagining Dave and Jacey, arms wrapped round each other, their limbs coiled together like a nest of pythons. And all the time my stomach ache is worsening. My belly is hard and full, as if something is going to burst. It's as if I've swallowed something small, like a pearl-sized grain of rice and it's swollen up with everything I've ever drunk and is pushing and pushing against my skin, trying to get out, shoving my insides right out of position.

The sound of my bedroom door opening wakes me. Jacey is standing there. It's about ten in the morning. I've forgotten it's Saturday and she doesn't have to work. Her face is like thunder, her hair wild and she looks like Medusa from Dad's favourite film *The Clash of the Titans*.

'You've been in my bedroom again, you little cow,' she hisses.

'I haven't.'

'You have. You've been in my jewellery box. Your sticky little paw prints are all over it. And you've taken my pearls. I'm going to tell Mum.'

'No, no, don't.' I struggle under my bedclothes, but my body is heavy and I can't move. I've got no energy. Overnight it has been sucked out of me.

'They're still in your room, under your bed. I'll mend them, honest I will.' My voice is harsh, doesn't sound a bit like me.

I ease myself out of bed and her face expression changes. She's gone white and her hair seems to have calmed down. It's then that I realise I'm sticky between my legs. I look down at myself and catch sight of the brown of dried blood, rich and dark against my pearly young thighs.

Marg Roberts

One hundred and eighty Anglo Saxon skeletons excavated

180 Anglo Saxon skeletons were discovered when underfloor heating was installed in Chapter House, at Worcester Cathedral.

whispering bones   waiting in line
singing stones   whispering
waiting in line   words sung
whispering   waiting in line
sung beneath tremulous diapason   whispering
waiting in line   below wall wash
blackened emptiness   whispering
whispering bones   waiting in line
old tyme words   whispering
while waiting in line   words hidden under stone
burned bones buried   waiting in line
whispering   words
slip like soup   sweet as mead
resurrected   whispering bones
waiting in line   black under stone
whisper words   sing secrets
stone bones filed   in line
held like an organ stop   washed, whispering
slow, singing, waiting   waiting in line
washed bones whispering   whispering bones

Lindsay Fursland

Hurricane Daughter

Forecast is you're imminent,
but neither of us wants to batten down
a single hatch or shield any window;
making landfall, you'll find open house,
be invited to blow us away.

The nurse subtitles
ultrasound's silent movie.
We catch first port-hole glimpses
from those early Apollos: beauty-shocked
we look homeward at the planet…

Argentina's foetal curve and curl,
The Andes' silver chain your backbone
down to Tierra del Fuego,
your once-upon-a-time tail;
and half a world away

your skull is in the cloudy Caribbean,
amazing brain, Amazon-veined,
brewing up a storm, vortexing an eye
composed about its spooky, low-pressure peace;
steadily you survey your options…

Nameless, but the greatest storms are always female.
Who can predict your trajectory?

Bognor Regis—1957

Photo. You carry me.
We squint at an out-of-shot
black and white, undesigner, fifties,
grey-frilled English Channel.
I'm just trying to like it, and do vaguely,
but you look pissed off at what you can see coming in:
the promise-breaking rollers;
the bicker of gulls; the dodgy ticker,
twenty years of pills; the three strokes;
the scrimped intimacies—all out of shot.

          and out of shot before I'm born you see
Icarian, hurricane-swallowing waves,
drinking charred heroics, wiping
cockpit-cocky, spitfire grins; you see
sacrificial waters; somewhere to bring
a future son.

          Out of shot, my ideal fragment...
two years later in a nook of St. Brelade,
postcard-ultramarine... I watch you
with the frown digitalis will unfurrow
bouncing stones, wristily flat-angling them.
Most bomb, but about one in six
kiss gravity bye bye—one two three
and shimmeringly brake
like neurons firing...

          But in shot, my new coat
makes me look cold. You ask:
Do you like the white horses?
Out of shot, greeny-brown froth
and a blustering East pours cold water on
your hopeful question; and my chilly
trying-to-smile answer almost drowns.

          I did! I always did. And as the semeny smell
of any seaside kids my old brain back
to toddler-hood, to being-in-arms-hood,
I wonder if you time-travelled too, out of shot,
even as you held me under that weather,
a sort of privacy invading itself.

Margaret Wilmot

Reading *Little Gidding* to my mother

reading to the memory
of my mother as well as to
this aged person smiling
at her daughter simply
because she loves her
and it's morning in the Sun Room—
reading how you had no purpose
or the purpose is beyond
the end you figured, reading
how this is the use of memory…
I glance to check because
you have been less than well, and your eyes
are utterly intent, still:
I turn my own eyes back, away—unable
to make these jumps in time
so easily. I can *imagine*
you are you again, but then,
a second's proof that my dream's true—
I hastily read on to keep
my tears at bay, how a people
without history is not redeemed from time…
Winter's thin light seeps through
the cottage pane as we sit here, in England…
So often it seems you have arrived
where you started, are leaning
on the unknown, remembered gate,
laughing at children's voices, laughing
delightedly in a condition
of complete simplicity
(costing not less than everything),
and all is well,
all manner of thing is well.

How from nothing

Dear Mimi, On the plane I read two books
of modern poetry and thought of you. I liked
District and Circle for all its layers, and how
from nothing he swells something huge.
I'm writing at my aunt's desk, looking out across
the view which was her world these last years.
She noticed the smallest things, would call out,
He's flying the Italian flag today!
I'd come, peer at a tiny flutter roofs away.
I can't find it now, have forgotten where
to look in this uneven scape of tarry squares.
Once we watched a living Edward Hopper, pale flesh
framed in his bleak light. These people who help us see.
I've found a postcard, hope the stamp is right.

Phil Madden

Taita de Carnivale calls

The Taita de Carnivale calls
to see if you have done well,
to see if your house is clean.
Then you will be invited
or else have hunger all the year.
And not be part of the Minga.
You will not be asked to help.
And no-one will help you.

Ambridge is interested
in a twinning arrangement.

Indian Expeditions

Visit the land of the bungee jumpers.
Go to London, the authentic heart of
their jungle. There are many tribes, and a clockwork leader.
Have your nails painted like the natives.
Experience the thrill of going deep in the earth with
many people in total silence. Enjoy their sacred dancing.
There will be flashing lights.

You may see machetes but they are not allowed.
The people are friendly as they take your money.
For the more adventurous there is bingo.

Losing Eden
Chloe George

Maria had lit a candle on the kitchen table, because the yoga teacher had said something about winter and fire and keeping flames burning. Light fell near the red apples in the bowl and she moved it nearer so the candle made a shining white dot on each.

Since they moved here there was time to contemplate the aesthetics of things, to pick up toys from the floor and put them inside the chest and close it; to turn the main light out and lean over to exchange it for the night-feed timbre of the side lamp; to tuck the welly boots in a neat row with their backs facing the half dark of the hall.

She thought about how it would be possible to stand there all day on the stone-flagged floor without anyone knowing, with the hulking trees in the copse outside as a watchful backdrop and the moon, like a shocked mouth, low in the daytime sky. She could stand unmoving until she had to pick the children up from school, and Jamie would come in and ask her what she did that day and she would say: I went to the shops, then I had a coffee, then I cleaned the bathroom and I put a wash on. Then I made soup. I sent some emails. But in truth she would stand still as a tree all day, and it would feel like she was squeezing out time. It would be strange that she would be the only person who knew what really happened in the interior of the house. And somehow being the only person to know this domestic secret seemed to make it less likely to have happened at all.

Della and Simon crashed through the kitchen and she remembered that it was Thursday and she had not yet taken them to school.

'How are you, how are you, how are you, how are, how are you, how are you, how are you, how are you,' Della sung to the tune of *Away In A Manger.* Simon joined in enthusiastically as they put on their boots. They are good children, Maria thought, the way they get themselves ready without being asked. Or perhaps they just want to get to school.

She followed them out of the door and into the car, as they continued the song without taking a breath. As she drove, she noticed the way the twigs stuck off the side of the trees like dead fingers, the fatalities of winter. She thought of the half-hearted London snow, the way it melted into an embarrassed pile of sludge, and then the downfall here, trapping them regularly in the house for days at a time in a strange, woolly silence. During bad weather one year, a man had walked into a local bar and shot himself in the head, someone had told her. The place had since closed. The sign was still outside; the dark oak chairs and tables, made for winter, still waiting around inside.

'Why don't you sing one of the other songs Della has been practicing for her assembly?' she suggested on the fifteenth rendition of their song.

The proposal took, this time, and the strange blend of Disney hits and odes to a generic God lasted all the way to the school entrance. She parked on the kerb like you weren't supposed to, got them out of the car and kissed them on their downy faces, like the other mothers did their children.

At the pharmacy, the woman in front of her was talking in low tones to the woman behind the counter. Maria tried not to listen. They eventually retired to the side room marked 'private', though it was glass-fronted and clearly framed the woman pointing to a clear patch on the side of her head where the hair had all come out. Maria looked away quickly. Hairs falling out. Falling out with each other. Falling out of sorts. It must be hard not to know when it will stop, Maria thought as she handed over her prescription. Whether it will grow back; whether it's just a light shower or the start of a fucking tsunami. Men lose their hair, though usually in a well-ordered, acceptable way, a slow progression with time to say goodbye. Trust women to malfunction in rude, unexplained bursts.

At home she showered and dried her hair carefully, looking at the roots in the mirror. They looked strong enough, for now. What about the rest of her? She had fought and fought to come here over the years, which must have taken resolve. She couldn't see much of that persistence in her face, but then persistence was not the same as strength. She had simply made herself unreasonable until Jamie agreed. Now, he said frequently 'I love it here'. We love it here. He was falling in love all the time and noticing nothing.

Jemma's cottage was grey stone, wild, sprawling, like all the places round here. Detached grade II listed farmhouse in a rural

106

situation with magnificent elevated views, the spec on their place had said. Three bedrooms, study/bed, bathroom, shower room, attic, cellar, garage. Sizeable outbuildings including barn, grainstore, workshop. Porch. Hayloft. Spring well supply.

There was the space, everywhere, the same space that she had craved. It turned out there was different types of space, though. Some of it sucked you in, some filled you up like a balloon and some of it made as if to drown you.

The garden path had crunchy gravel, 'burglar proof' Jemma had said, the first and only other time Maria had been there during a moment short on conversation, where the topic of gravel had seemed a welcome thirty second respite from silence. She enjoyed the moment of walking up the drive, before the talking came. It would be nice to stay crunching on the gravel. Simon would like it. He would crunch and crunch, the worst burglar in the world.

'Maria!' a voice behind her. It was one of the women. She felt a stab of panic as she tried to remember the woman's name. Rebecca Martha Astrid Zoe Sara Lelaina Debbie India Rose Melanie Lara Sophie Asha? She said an extra friendly, familiar 'hello!' to compensate. They all seemed to resemble each other: dark hair, good skin, pretty smile, well-tailored bohemian clothes. Top knots mixed with a man's Barbour, oversized woollen wraps, thick tights and biker boots. Chanel lipstick. Somehow outside of and bigger and better than fashion.

'How are you Maria? All settled in now? Boxes all unpacked?'

They were unable to remember that they had this same conversation every time.

'Good thanks. Settling in fine. How are you?'

'Oh great, you know. Plodding along. Good that you're all settled in, you'll love it here'. Everyone said this to Maria. You'll love it. It's wonderful here. The scenery. The sense of community. The local produce.

Jemma opened the door. 'Cara and Maria!' Jemma's expression suggested she was genuinely enjoying the moment more than she had ever enjoyed anything. 'I'm so glad you could come!'

'So glad *I* could come,' smiled Maria, because in the world there are many lies.

The floors in the hall were stripped white wood, the hall bare except for a 1930s side table and a painting of a brutal seascape on the wall. With all the money in the world, I could never make my house look like this, thought Maria. I would get the wrong decade, the wrong floral, overload the walls. Where do they get this knowledge, this capital? In which magazines do they find the information? How do they know that they are the *right* magazines?

In the lounge, a woman was emptying out carefully iced cupcakes with violet icing from a Tupperware container to a china plate. Maria was glad she left the Mr Kiplings at home. An unwritten rule was that all objects must complement the ideal of rural bohemian fun. Looking at the woman briefly, Maria swore she saw a bald patch near her ear and wondered if it was the woman from the pharmacy. But when she looked back it was a small pink flower in her hair.

'You can't just be a cake shop anymore,' the woman was saying to the person next to her. 'You have to be a brand, even out here. That was our thinking with the street party and the blog. It's personality behind the company, making people feel they've got something to be loyal to. Taste and quality come first, of course, but that's not enough these days. And it means the opportunities are endless, you can keep *diversifying.*'

'You're right,' sighed the other woman. 'There's so much to think about. We've finally got the website sorted out, and Jack's sister is revamping our visual identity.'

Maria had perched on the last available space on a sofa. She couldn't think of a way to break into the conversation, and the women were keeping their eyes on each other. She turned her head the other way. The women on that side were in a similarly awkward position, so that she could see the back of one's head and the other was hidden from her eyeline. The woman's hair was thick and lustrous, a sturdy hairline with no tell-tale gaps.

'I wouldn't say fat exactly', she heard one of them say, 'she's just big boned.'

'Yes,' another said in reply, 'it's not actual *fat* is it; she's quite *lean,* but definitely not small either.' Then she laughed.

Maria got up again; she wondered if she could leave so soon.

'Maria! Come and have a cup of tea,' Jemma called from the side of the room. Maria felt sure people had started looking at her. Walking across the room felt like picking her way across slippery stepping stones. She picked up the cup with one hand only around the top rim (why? she had never held a cup like this before) and immediately knew it was too heavy and was going to slip from her fingers. It bounced beautifully off the table and spilt all over the white sofa.

'Oh god,' said Jemma weakly, a blush rising in her cheeks like paint percolates through water. It went quiet. The cake shop woman stared.

'Oh god,' echoed Maria. 'I'm so sorry.'

Someone had run to get a cloth. Loads of cold water, someone said. White wine vinegar, said someone else. Detergent. Maria waited for someone to say that it was ok, that it was only an accident. But instead there were a lot of concerned faces. It was as if she had unbuttoned her jeans and taken a piss on the distressed floor. She remembered what the woman in the hospital had said to her after Della was born, when it all started: don't worry dear; most people are broken up on the inside or the out.

She used her second trip back to the kitchen with the cloth as a reason to stay in the there. It was more manageable. Wipeable surfaces.

'Don't worry, these things happen', a woman said. Finally. We all piss on the floor from time to time.

Back home, she picked up a pen and notepad and sat at the kitchen table.

'Bacon', she wrote. 'Milk. Clean bathroom. Door curtain.' She put a line through clean bathroom, as she had done this yesterday. She felt afraid to continue writing, because you could carry on planning things to do forever and never ever stop.

She noticed food marks splashed on the hob and the wall and slowly started to wash them off, the straightforward smell of disinfectant comforting her. Twice she mistook poppy seeds floating in the washing up bowl as moving bugs out of the corner of her eye. But they lay dead in the sink.

She had cleaned two rooms, but the stains seemed to be increasing, not disappearing, when she heard Jamie's key opening the door.

'Hello!' as he threw his coat down onto the kitchen table and looked through the post. Recently all his sentences sounded like they had exclamation marks at the end of them. Had he always sounded like this or was it a mark of his contentedness at their new life? Even when he said he was tired, or hungry, or that his mother's cancer had come back, she could hear the exclamation mark. Knackered! Starving! Cancer! They hung in the air like bad jokes. 'Where are the kids?'

She stared at him, blinked. 'What?'

'I thought they'd be back from school by now', he said loudly. There was a small giggle from the hallway.

'Oh. I don't know, what do you think's happened to them?' Go through the motions.

Della and Simon bundled through. Jamie opened a bottle of wine, poured it into glasses. The glugging made her shudder.

'Good day was it? Have fun with the girls?' He was picking at pistachio nuts and looking over the paper. When you come home from work you have something to relax *from*.

'Lots of fun.' There was new pleasure in lying, in saying the opposite and seeing how long he would fail to observe it. 'Really fun.' His body had changed in the country. He went for runs, played rugby. He looked healthy and far away.

'Great.' He looked up and smiled. 'Cheers,' he said, tipping his glass. He'd said to her after they'd moved: You were right. Good call baby.

She moved his coat off the table and into the place where it belonged. At the window there was a figure walking past the house and away from the village. She drew the curtains shut.

Della and Simon weren't at school the next day so it must have been a Saturday, though she couldn't be sure and she didn't dare ask. Within ten minutes of getting up their toys were forested across the floor of the kitchen and their shrieks were getting louder and louder. The sound of Jamie's car died away. She couldn't remember where he said he was going.

She lit a fire and put the guard in front of it. She wrote on Facebook: 'Snowing outside, cuddling up with Della and Simon in front of fire', because writing it seemed a way of keeping human. After a while she checked the page. There were two thumbs up under her statement. But the sentence seemed to get more and more concave as the minutes went by.

As she walked through the hall she saw the front door was open and heard Simon gabbling to someone. By the time Maria got to the door, he was alone and looking out to the road.

'Who was it?' she said sharply.

'A lady,' he said, hopping on one foot then the other.

'Who? What did she want?'

'I am Spiderman', shouted Simon.

'Come in. It's too cold. Don't open the front door without asking me.'

She put their film on and lay on the other sofa and when she woke up it had finished and started again. They were watching, wordless, their fingers in their mouths. She was felled timber with more falling on top.

Two days later she couldn't work out why they were still at home until Della told her 'it's half term, silly,' and she patted Maria's head as she stood on the arm of the sofa. Maria looked at her. Hair curly like a silky bird's nest. Apple cheeks. 'Thank you,' she said softly.

But later they were screaming and shouting and Simon was calling her and she shut the door on them and pulled the bolt across and stayed in the kitchen and hours must have passed because the light had gone and eventually she could hear Della crying and she ran into the bedroom and picked her up and they looked at her like they were frightened. And then she bathed them and put the clothes to wash and let them eat too much chocolate and kept thinking sorry, sorry but she didn't say it in case they told Jamie.

After they were in bed she combed her hair in the bathroom and was sure more was coming out than usual. She threw the stray hairs in the bin and cried. She woke in the night to touch it gingerly, put her hand on the pillow dreading what she might find.

In the night the mice were scratching behind the walls, and her heart lurched every time she heard them. Once there was an almighty crash and her mind rushed to picture the size of the rodent that could make such a sound. But it must have been a cat or a fox in the garden. She sank back down, sweating, wide awake. In the end she got up to do some chores, and when Jamie came in she was cleaning on her hands and knees in the bathroom. The stains on the bath wouldn't disappear, however much she scrubbed.

A week later the woman was back in the pharmacy: the patch was getting bigger. The pharmacist was talking to her about Nutracare or Naturacare or Follicare. Maria tried not to look at her.

'Are you sure you're alright?' she could hear her mother saying down the telephone one evening.

The mornings looked more like dusk, until she realised they were dusk.

She woke one night and thought: I am so tired of failing to fill up the space inside me. I am just shifting abacus bead back and

111

forth.

She moved quietly across the landing, pushed open the children's door noiselessly. She got into bed with Della, took up the space behind her, pressed into her body so there was nothing between them. She squeezed the little body hard as if she could move her sweetness into her own mind.

The moonlight came in the gap between the curtains and fell on the wooden floor and the rocking horse, the clothes on the floor and the plug for the lamp with its teeth facing up into the sky. She could move in to the scene and tidy it, leave things prettier than before. But what would it change? They had moved because she had started to hate the city, its propensity to come alive, unpredictable, like a violent beast. But maybe you can't stem violence, not anywhere.

She shut her eyes tight, listening to Della breathe. She opened them to look over at Simon, the small bump in the bed, the hot face on the pillow. The bed was flat. She got a sense of its temperature from its emptiness, and that was all she could think for perhaps thirty seconds—its coldness, how icy it would be to slide into, how she wanted to get him a hot water bottle, fill it tenderly, tuck him in and touch the head that was the place where all his funny thoughts and words started.

And then she was sprinting to the front door which was wide open and all she could think of was good mothers and pills in the bathroom cabinet like malign soldiers and she ran outside as Jamie shouted from the bedroom and Della started to wail as she ran out to the woods, and it felt like being blind, blind, with the dark blowing in and the shocked mouth moon and the night filling her ears like a busy history.

Gillian Laker

Grave Amber

I am the tear
that fell through time
rolling the memory of giants
into a ball
I am a pledge
sentient and arboreal

Alice—you might say
on the far side of the glass
ice cracking for the
Baltic to return me

washed
worn
a play of infant bubbles
at my core

and destined for a while
to mourn the bones
and celebrate
the strange supremacy
of this mute Triassic shrew

Stuart Duncan

How the Rooftop Speaks

The city lost its voices long ago:
human shadows drowned by
marketing and ambulances
shunting people dreaming
in unheard languages.
Crow calls rule the black
steel of the gleaming trees,
metallic behind the rooftop
monuments of satellite TVs.
Refusing to be scripted,
an aerial points a wash of pink
across December afternoons,
naming something I have lost
in the silence of a room.

Stone Song

The geologist's rod
taps blunt Morse
from stones six feet
below the grassy peat.

Now they sing louder
than the near waves,
in tongues of those
who spoke them into place:

They are tuning forks
across the cliff tops.
Goose-pimpled on
a dark horizon,
    we hear centuries of us speak.

Sue Moules

A Brush Stroke

There's sheen and shadow in her hair
as she lifts bacon from the packet
places it on the grill.
The rattle of turquoise and gold plates,
light shines through the porcelain
moons curved with sea waves.

We have walked through the sea,
ransacked our feet with sand
A line of grit surfs the floor,
our pockets tumble shells.

The dog digs its head
into the food bowl.
The radio brings in the outside world,
as we go back and back,
Sunday morning, a church bell in the air,
the smell of bacon, the richness of coffee.

This moment in her kitchen;
she turns and smiles,
a tenderness like a picture
she might one day paint.

Wreaths

In Brondeifi churchyard
we'd found dried hydrangeas
under glass bell jars,
lifted the lids to let spiders
and condensation escape.

Victorian wreaths, delicate,
like faded embroidery samplers
not like the modern ones
blocks of white chrysanthemums
MUM or DAD, or the sad echo of a name.

When you died it was November
no wild flowers except the twigs and berries
we cut from your garden,
my garden,
the greenery you'd always loved.

Your brother sent a white lily tribute,
your cousin yellow and blue irises,
but I remembered those glass domed
brittle faded hydrangeas
we'd come across on our walks so long ago.

Green Feathers
Gina Challen

Tom looked at a large bar of fruit and nut chocolate and a packet of white chocolate buttons. He couldn't make up his mind which he wanted. It was a hard decision because there wasn't enough time to consider it properly. Tom didn't like rushing, that was when you made mistakes, and mistakes could hurt. He tucked the shoe box he was carrying under his arm and looked at the money in his hand. The money made him uneasy, but he thought he had enough.

The sign above the window said, 'Mr Smith's Sweetie Box'. The shop was small and usually quiet, and Tom liked quiet places. There was a rundown homeliness hanging over the place. Its magazines were faded and sun-bleached and the sell-by-dates on the sweets, almost forgotten. He wasn't sure if the old man behind the counter was Mr Smith. Sometimes people said one thing to you, and meant another.

Mr Smith was always polite to him, said, 'Good Morning, Thomas. How are you today?' and stepped slightly backwards. Tom hated questions. They needed answers that he didn't have. He tried not to mind Mr Smith, and each time answered, 'F… F… Fine.' Once he tried to say 'Fine, thanks, Mr Smith.' Mr Smith always chatted to him when he went in. About the weather, or the Youth-of-Today, or the birds he fed on his bird table. Tom thought he might be lonely. Old people often were.

There was something reassuring about a whole bar of chocolate. Solid. It was finished and complete. And Tom loved fruit and nut. Almonds and raisins. Each one a tiny little surprise. It made him think of hiding places. He liked to suck off all the chocolate then he was left with the nuts and raisins sitting in his mouth, ready to be crunched up. Like bones. This made him laugh. Out loud. He considered explaining to Mr Smith, who must have heard, but the old man turned away and straightened some cigarettes on the shelves behind the counter. The white chocolate buttons were slippy in their packet. Very slightly waxy he thought. He didn't want to choose the wrong chocolate, but you mustn't be too long choosing. It was all so difficult. He bought the fruit and nut.

Tom always walked home through the park on good days. He liked to see the children playing. On exceptionally good days he liked to sit by the trees, at the green plastic picnic tables, and eat his chocolate bar. It was a good place to watch. The picnic tables, like the trees, hadn't been there that long. Tom wasn't keen on the benches. He thought the heavy duty resin made his legs sweat. Even on chilly days.

It had been an exceptionally good day and when Tom left the shop that Tuesday, he had the chocolate bar in the left hand pocket of his coat. He could feel the weight of the chocolate pulling the side of the jacket down, making him feel happy and slightly lopsided. With each step he could feel the corner of the bar push into the flesh of his thigh.

It was the shoe box he carried that made walking such a problem. Tom held it in both hands, close to his chest. Elbows bent and tucked in. Every few steps, he pushed his right elbow slightly downward to feel the bulge of the chocolate, pushed deep inside his coat pocket. It wasn't straightforward, but he needed to know the chocolate was safe. It made the contents of the cardboard box slide towards the right, then back again as he pulled his elbow back. Every time this happened he heard a slight scratching sound.

Tom tried to keep the box as upright as possible. He was worried that the continual movement would damage them. Tom wanted to lift the corner of the lid a little bit and see if he could spot any breakages. But you must never open a box. No matter what happened. It slowed him down on his way to the park.

It was definitely a chocolate-in-the-park day, and Tom felt overwhelmingly pleased with how it was turning out. There had been the possibility that things weren't going to go as planned; something he found happened quite a lot to him. He always tried very hard to do the right thing. You have to. From the minute Tom had left the house he chanted the list of instructions over and over. Under his breath. There's trouble if you forget. He had been very apprehensive as he withdrew the cash, looking around to make absolutely sure nobody was near. Exactly like he had been told. He worried the machine may decide not to give him any money. After all it wasn't really his. So he held his breath as the machine whirred.

Tom had quickly counted the notes, folded them over, and

thrust them deep down into an inside pocket. All the way to the meeting place he chanted the list of instructions. He even spun round a few times just to check no one was following him. You should always check no one is following you. The money in his pocket frightened him. It was heavy, sitting close against his heart.

It was slightly early when Tom arrived, and as he stood waiting, he clenched his hands into fists, his fingernails cutting crescents into his flesh. Over and over, he chanted the instructions, rocking gently backwards and forwards. He was sure it was the right place. He was sure nobody had followed him. You should always check. As soon as Tom spotted the man walking towards him, carrying a canvass shopping bag, he guessed it must be the right one. But he knew he mustn't move. And he didn't. Tom stood very still and waited to see if the man would come up to him and speak to him. You can't speak to them. Ever.

Tom didn't check the box before handing over the money. He didn't open it. He just thrust the cash forward in one hand and took the box in the other. The trembling of his hand had made the contents subtly shift. Back and forth. That made him almost drop the box. He thought they were breathing. Now he had them, Tom had just wanted to get away. He had done everything, exactly like the instructions said. Now he could go and buy his chocolate.

In the park his usual table was occupied by a group of young, chattering mothers with babies perched on their knees. The table was spread with containers of food, cartons of juice and cardboard cups of coffee. Their other young children ran about, intermittently swooping on the table to snatch up cake and crisps. Tom stood under the trees watching.

The women carried on talking. Tom couldn't quite hear what they said. There were two facing him, and they darted glances his way. Children ran round in dizzying circles, shouting and calling. Tom could feel the weight of the chocolate in his pocket. He stared at the children. He didn't have time for this. One young woman reached for her coffee, and when she pushed her sunglasses onto her head, her eyes momentarily caught Tom's. Startled, she dropped her gaze to the shoe box held tight in his hands. Turning back, she spoke quickly to her friends.

Babies were swiftly strapped into pushchairs. Coffee swallowed. Food and drink packed into bags. Crumbs brushed to the grass. One called to the playing children, gathering them to her. Another grabbed the rubbish for the bin. As they moved off, holding their older children by the hand, Tom sat himself at the empty table. The bench felt warm. Trapped body heat and a slight smell of citrus perfume. He was faintly unsettled.

He put down the box and lined up the edges of the lid with the grooves on the table, twisting it slightly back and forth until it felt perfect. It was impossible to tell if anything was broken. Breakages would be very bad. Tom ran his hands over the lid without touching it.

You should never open the box. Once. Twice. The third time his thumb and index finger darted downwards and pulled up the edge of the lid. He breathed in the small amount of stale, shut in air. He looked at the blurred, dark shapes inside. He let his breath out in a long sigh. Nothing was damaged. And they were very beautiful. Tom didn't touch them. He knew better than that.

There were no children to watch, but Tom thought he might still eat his chocolate. He could see a group of teenagers in the distance, laughing and smoking. They were far enough away not to bother him. As he pulled the fruit-and-nut from his jacket, he caught a flash of colour under the bench. Red. A baby's shoe. Tom reached down for it. The shoe sat small and exquisite in his hand. The soft red leather was uncreased. He smoothed his fingertip gently over the swell of the toe. He felt honoured to hold such a thing. He placed it tenderly next to the box, along with the chocolate bar.

Running his thumbnail along the groove in the chocolate, Tom broke a piece free. An almond poked from the edge. He smiled. As he sucked the gluey chocolate his tongue pushed into a hole left from a raisin. His mouth felt viscous and faintly oily. He closed his eyes. Piece by piece Tom ate his chocolate.

'Excuse me, that's mine.'

Tom's body stiffened. His eyes jumped open.

'I said that's mine.'

One of the young mothers stood before him. Even without her children, he knew it was the same woman. Even with her sunglasses hiding her eyes. Tom recognised the citrus perfume.

'You've found it. Thanks... I mean... I'm very grateful... Thanks.' And her hand reached out towards the table.

'No. D... D... Don't t... t... touch.' Tom stood. He jerked forward, his arm out. 'N... N... Never touch. Tha... Tha... That's v... v... very b... b... bad.'

She flinched as the force of Tom's hand knocked her arm away.

Glaring at Tom, the young woman stepped back. She saw the spit speckling the front of his jacket. As Tom stood, she looked around quickly. In the distance, the group of teenagers were beginning to break up. They threw their cigarettes to the ground, and crushed them under their twisting heels. They squeezed each others' shoulders and exchanged friendly punches, with promises to meet later. As they began to move away, the young woman shouted out. The teenagers turned and stared. The noise settled over Tom, holding him, momentarily, completely still. The young women, Tom, the teenagers, they were all caught together by the sound of the shout. Tom gasped. He reeled backwards away from the noise, and finding his legs caught by the bench, sat down heavily.

His sudden weight caused the bench and table to lift slightly at one end, freeing it from the hard ground. It dropped back down with a groan. Chocolate wrappers fluttered onto the grass. Tom felt the sweat break out on his face as he watched the cardboard box and the shoe slide towards the ground with the table's seesaw movement. When the table levelled, the box settled back into its resting place, but the shoe carried on sliding and tumbled slowly over the edge. Dust flew up, blurring the soft, red leather, as it lay, upside down and vulnerable, in the dirt.

The teenagers ran towards them. Shouting. Footsteps. Dust beaten up from the ground. Tom sat. Perfectly still. His hand on the top of the box. You can't ever let anyone touch the box. Understand. Tom looked hard at her; he didn't know what to do. The sunglasses shielded her eyes. When the teenagers arrived, throwing questions at them both, she reached up and pushed the glasses onto her head.

'Miss, you alright?'

'You ok?'

'Mate, what're you doing?'

The young woman, dropped her gaze from Tom, stepped backwards into the group, and the teenagers closed around her.

'What's he doing, sitting there?'

'Like, seen him before. He watches.'

'He's a right weirdo.'

Tom flinched, as their voices rose louder. He lurched out from the table, and stood in front of them, his hands loose by his sides.

Tom felt the teenagers crowd towards him. He moved away, then realised the shoe box was out of his reach. He shuffled sideways. He mustn't let it out of his sight. Never.

'Mate, wot y'doing?'

'Wants the box, don't he. What's in it, perv?'

And one youth, his pierced lip curled up, whipped forward to snatch up the box. He quickly grabbed at it but misjudged the distance. His knuckles slid across the cardboard, and he was left with only the lid held between his tattooed fingers, whilst the rest of the box spiralled across the table and over the edge.

As the contents hit the ground, the group fell silent.

'Oh, no. No.' The young woman whimpered and stumbled backwards. The dark shapes rolled slowly over and settled, resting one against the other.

'What the…?'

'Jesus.'

'What's … Oh my God. P… er… v?'

Three small birds nestled amongst the dust and crumbs on the ground, their green feathers sleek against their bodies. Shiny as new leaves. Minute black eyes, glinting in the light.

'Are they like dead, or what?' The tattooed boy gently pushed at the nearest bird with his toe, wiping a half circle of dust from his trainer with the tiny body. Tom tried to shout out, but his whispered cry was lost amongst the rustling of jackets as they all leaned forward.

'Yeah, dead, mate.'

Laughing, the boy kicked out. The bird spun through the air and landed, with a small escape of dust, next to the chocolate wrappers. Nervous giggles broke from the teenagers. Another one kicked out, and the birds, like emerald shuttlecocks, were rallied back and forth. Tom flinched with every kick.

'No… no… no.' Tom began to shriek. This wasn't meant to happen. He hadn't been told this might happen. It meant trouble. Big trouble. Smack-you-hard-in-the-mouth trouble. *Don't ever let anyone touch the box open the box the box the box don't ever the box anyone touch the box.* Tom hunched his shoulders and threw his arms around his head. His legs buckled and he collapsed onto the ground. Tom drew his knees up to his chest and lay, perfectly still, his head in the nest of his arms.

Everything stopped. A small broken body rolled across the dirt and rested against the foot of the picnic table. Bright feathers gently floated to the ground. Tom began to cry. Little moans shook his body. He inched his way across the grass until he lay, curled into a ball, underneath the picnic table. Amongst the chocolate wrappers.

Without looking at Tom, the young woman darted forward, snatched up the red baby's shoe, and clutched it tightly in her hand. She walked swiftly away. Back to her group of waiting friends just inside the park gates. She held it up as she reached them. A perfect little red shoe.

The teenagers looked at each other. One by one they backed away from the picnic table. They turned and began to jog slowly towards the park gates. They found a different place to smoke.

Two streets away a man sat in a room surrounded by birds. Branches covered in finches and bee eaters. Bright macaws on perches. A powerful eagle with its wings outstretched. All silent. Going nowhere. In the kitchen a board sat on the table, next to silver pins. The man waited for his son to come home. He kept looking at the clock. His hands, on the arms of his chair were clenched into fists.

Gradually the sun moved round in the afternoon sky. The light shone bright in the park. It shone on the green feathers. They glittered like tiny jewels.

Anthony Costello

On Becoming 'Glenn Ford'

This motel room
reminds me of Nabokov,
a king-sized bed
and curtains drawn at the edges

                         revealing

strips of virgin lawn;
or Glenn Ford
stepping on the verandah
to strike a match
and blow the clouds of his evening pipe…
…thinking of nothing…
…then…
thinking of becoming an actor
…then…
thinking of nothing in particular, at all

Maria Louise Apichella

Honey

That morning a jar
was knocked
and toast-flecked honey
inched across the breakfast table
like dense sunlight;
anyone else would have
scooped it back in,
ashamed to waste
in a gnawed up world.
Yet he let it spill,
washed out the jar
poured in new amber
a slow
coming sweetness,
a kiss.

Psalm 1

It reads: Blessed are they who are picky
with friends; who turn people like peaches in the hot
slant of a fly-flicked market.

They are a flask of chilled water, poured
into empty cups. A bowl of washed apples
next to sticks of pink candy floss. A stone
in our shoe, slowing us down, a splinter
of mirrors, our view.

*

What is this word 'Blessed?'
a word l finger about, thick,
segments of oranges
arranged on a blue plate.
I spit sour flesh, pith, pips for the
juice, chewable drinkable sun.

*

Who are these *wicked* I must avoid to be *blessed*?
Is David wicked? Am *I* blessed?

Father, you are made of love in all its bitter green flavours.
This I've know from childhood. You make and re-make
all things willing to be touched.
Do not make me reduce my heart, eyes, thought to
us   *them*.

I know no evil in this corner of Wales.
I have done no serious harm with these hands.
Yet in my mind I have
stultified   cheated   denied.

Sarah

Each night anchored
below her man she sways
like a gale
she howls. In the morning
he surveys the damage.   Nothing.
          His palms press inner hush. In the stillness
          no life
          kicks.
His arms cradle a woman bare as a basket
where she holds
the love of a man she loves,
a flat with space for more.

Don't the lemons look luminous
in her dark wooden bowls?
Their scent fills her ever-moving kitchen,
washes everything.
Lemons bitter as light,
sweeter than light.

God drums inside her. Lives in the shapes
between her lips.
A note,   a reverberation,
small enough to fit in the fist
of her heart without exploding
like white noise behind her ribs.

And this holds her in place,
keeps her
                    laughing.

The Book of Euclid
Patrick Riordan

It was widely anticipated that on his coming of age my father would inherit the farm, but let's not beat about the bush, his heart was not in the land. He needed something more challenging than a horse drawn plough, something more complex than crop rotation, with more intelligence than sheep, sweeter than pig or poultry. To a lad of tender years who'd excelled to no purpose at school, amazing his Master with his skill as a geometer, the farm was nothing if not a burden. The terrible prospect of a lifetime.

He began to shirk his responsibilities. Sleeping late, going missing across the county, agonizing his way from pub to pub, earning for himself a reputation as a right roaring boozer until at seventeen his exasperated father disinherited him.

'An ultimatum is it, Da?' he croaked, stroking the farm dog that had run out to greet the prodigal's return.

'The only decision to be made is do I kick you up the arse or hit you across the skull with a shovel. Now get out! Don't come back!'

Three quarters of a century later I regard my arrival in the country (albeit a different landscape, a different nation) married to Alice, a sheep-farmer's daughter, as the completion of an orbit begun when my grandfather's boot came in contact with my father's backside; the conversation that never took place; the understanding and compromise my ancestors were unable to reach and as a profound appreciation of the geometers' mysterious arts.

For some time Alice and I have slept apart. Our single beds the significant if only recent manifestation of a longstanding division of thoughts. Lately we've taken to sleeping in separate rooms. Practical reasons are given, veils of silence only half-believed. Last night however, we slept again like we used to. Shoulder to shoulder beneath the same covers. This morning I woke up wondering if I'd slept at all.

I crawl from bed without straightening and dress hastily for outside, throwing on two of everything against the cold. My breath glows like a torch beam in front of me as I unlatch the bedroom door and creep downstairs to the next disaster whereupon I am immediately reminded why she stole into my bed. No electricity.

'Light,' she murmured when there was only darkness. 'Scared,' she added boldly, showing no sign of fear. 'And cold,' she conceded burgling my bodies heat.

With the wires down and no juice through the switch for the foreseeable future we must resort to the primitive and boil up a kettle on the stove. It takes an age and to produce sufficient heat I must burn more logs. The wood situation is desperate. Like a witness from a preceding generation Samson the dog, rolled up with its snout under its tail, watches me and grumbles at my inadequacy.

Outside the first light of day is a silent, pagan white. The air is moist. I cross to the shed and chop the last ration of logs. The thud of the axe echoes around the yard. It's not enough to break a sweat. If it wasn't so blasted cold this primitive life would be healthy.

While I'm waiting for the kettle to warm I splash a coat of limewash on the pantry wall; a job I started to save my bacon and made a pig's ear of in the gloom last night. A 'saved bacon, pig's ear' pun smartens in my mind with each swathe and swipe of the brush. I wonder if I should tax her with words so early in the day. For the first time this morning I can feel a tingle of warmth through my veins.

I'm feeling mellow when the kettle lid rattles and I can leave a mug of tea billowing like a volcano on the floorboards beside her. I would've liked to warm it up with a tot of something kindly, but a bottle of whiskey bought for rare celebrations, I left at work.

She's awake, of course, but chooses not to acknowledge my choppings and changings. She turned in well after midnight miserable and forlorn. A faint smell of the yard on her hands; a whiff of the slow witted farm-boy in her tangled hair.

We returned to my father's disinheritance when I was five years old, his first homecoming since my grandfather died. The welcome was muted. He hadn't made it to the funeral. At the time these issues passed over my head. Now I'm dazzled by recollections of a grieving family holiday in which my father figures only as a muted voice and my mother as a shadow of herself. I remember my grandmother being continually tearful and arguments ceased abruptly to watch me pass through the room; the old farm dog in trail. Not a care in the world between us. To this day I can smell cut turf blocks baking in the sun, the dairy, the limewash and home-cured bacon frying in the pan.

She makes up a bucket of powdered milk at the big scullery sink. The number of orphaned lambs to be nursed increases nightly. A dozen quart size drinking bottles, rubber teats, caps have been soaking overnight in a disinfected tub. Her hands are raw, her cuffs wet and cold. Already she's wearing a scruffy woollen bonnet with the flaps dangling down over her ears. Alarmingly it doesn't look out of place on her or in our kitchen.

I go on about this and that. I can see she's preoccupied with her own thing and not listening, but I rattle on regardless for my own benefit. At lambing time breakfast is a precious hour reserved for talking. When I return this evening she'll be outside nourishing, bedding down and being a midwife to her flock.

Before she goes outside she armours herself in industrial overalls, yellow leggings and an unflinching waterproof coat on top of a double wrapping of thermals. She scrunches to the door sounding like a bowl of breakfast cereal. All that shows of the girl I married and dragged along with me on this futile tragic orbit are sleep eyes, red nose and her swollen fingers. She ties the woolly flaps under her chin and hears only what she wants to hear. I can't resist mild provocations before helping her on with her wellies; an awkward and exaggerated proximity, manoeuvring ourselves like coy new lovers.

'And your gloves?'

'What gloves? I don't have any gloves.'

'I can't believe you're not wearing gloves.'

'I'm in and out of water all day, it's never practical '

'You should buy some. Look in at the Farmers Co-op. See what they've got for you.'

'When do I get the chance... anyway, you should talk.'

'I don't need gloves. Not like you. When I get back tonight I'm going to turn out your cupboards and find the ones I bought two Christmases ago. Remember? They were a good pair. Cost an arm and a leg. They must be somewhere around here. I can't see them being ditched.' It's in her cupboards and secret places I find the things that once meant something; the once essential cogs in her machine: the buttons to shirts, clasps to bracelets, letters to

131

sweethearts.

The clock begins a long civilised chime and like robots we make our independent moves. We come together to kiss, but there's not enough skin to engage so we bump together blisslessly; two over-inflated pre-programmed dolls. I open the door. She hesitates then ducks into the icy blast. The stove putters beneath the kettle. I bolt up and draw the curtain behind her. The dog stirs, grumbles then returns to worldly contemplations.

Before leaving I scribble out a note. This is how we communicate. It tells her only what she knows: that I've chopped the last logs; that I've loaded the wood basket; that the outside toilet is frozen and I've tidied up the scullery wall. I write to her, she writes to me. I jot down what I've done. She prefers to tell me how, with so much to be done, she'll never be able to fill her quart pot of daily tasks in the pint glass of time available. Her mind has been hi-jacked by measuring cups, comparisons and reason.

Half an hour later after watching the dog take a turn around the yard, I set out for work only to find that the car won't start. Such events have been known to destroy lives. She grumbles and growls like a startled cat until petrol floods the carburettor and that's that. I resolve to the inevitable; three downhill miles walking at an angry pace. Angry thoughts reflecting my impatience with machines; angry thoughts fuelled by glimpses of my weatherproof wife; angry thoughts seeing Riff-raff, the slow-witted farm boy grinning at her side; angry thoughts anyway.

'Riff-raff, who's Riff-raff? His name's Ralph and he works for Uncle Ivan. He's the one dipping his hand in his pocket. We should be grateful.'

'Riff-raff.'

'No, Ralph. It's Ralph. Uncle Ivan said he could spare him for a few weeks to give me a hand through lambing. He knows it's a difficult time for us and to be honest Ralph's been a godsend. I don't know what we'd have done without him.'

'Riff-raff.'

'Why won't you call him Ralph?'

Gradually I'm pacified by the falling landscape and the steady lick of boots hitting a frozen stream of asphalt. On both sides of the lane spread vast acres of fields, some ploughed to reveal a stony soil breaking down beneath elongated caps of frost. The majority, however, put to grass. In the latter enclosures my wife's dismal sheep hobble miserably over the bleached out, lifeless

132

grasses. As I pass they stop grazing and stare at me inquisitively.

I slow down past the quarry entrance. Blasting times posted. The red flags show that explosions are imminent. I feel the earth tremble and watch sides of a cliff shatter. The bu-boom follows on as a tremor vibrates the soles of my feet. Another. Boom-bu-boom and a dense mustard coloured cloud expands, filling the quarry to its brim with choking particles of dust and gravel. Far below a faint siren calls out the all clear.

A mammy's boy, he was, my father, or so I'm told. I'm led to believe he left home aged eighteen with a flea in his ear. According to one source all he had to call his own were the clothes he stood up in and his school prize, a Book of Euclid wrapped in a brown paper parcel. On this harsh morning I'm feeling a strong affinity with my father. We are like two stones embedded in the same wall. It goes beyond looking like, acting like, sounding like or even feeling like. What I'm getting at is a communion of spirits. Body, mind, heart and soul until finally we become that person fully. My father never returned to the rural way of life. Nor can I recall him asking me to complete his circle, his orbit for him, although the Euclidean symbolism would have excited him. As I walk to work I have an overwhelming sensation I am following in his footsteps. Walking away from the farm, as he had done; the clothes I'm wearing the only outdoors clothes I possess; and then the images of a beleaguered family in postures of disapproval. If I'd been carrying anything at all to compare with his precious parcel it'd be in the shape of my packed lunch, but I'm not. First prize for guessing I've left my crib on the kitchen table. No prize at all for a picture of Samson up on his hind legs at the table scoffing the lot.

It could've been shock that made my father head off in a westerly direction towards Galway city, when everything in the country lay to the east. However when his chosen highway encountered the ocean he was pleased as punch that he was close enough to home to hear a mother's call if and when it was made. He reckoned he could be back by her side in a shot, but after two weeks stifling silence from home he bothered to unpack his canvas bag. By that time there was work for him in a Hotel—advertised as the last watering hole before America—and he'd managed to soft-soap the landlady into letting him live in. Three months later he was off again. Out on his arse with reasons of etiquette given. He was a young man that's all; learning the ropes in life

On to Dublin where he was taken on at the Castle. Dublin was a honey pot for minor clerks and civil servants and men like himself with nothing to lose who enjoyed the sociability of a drink. But like many another he couldn't settle. England beckoned.

In a dockside public house, the night before he embarked, he was given a five pound note and instructions to deliver a package to O'Connor in Liverpool. There'd be a further fifteen on the other side of the water if everything went to plan. It did. Twenty pounds better off, he rubbed his hands with glee and headed for the nearest Bar. It wasn't until the awful awakening that he discovered his school prize gone and what he'd hung onto was the intended object of transfer; a British Army service revolver. The following night he was arrested for being drunk and combative in the middle of St. George's Square. The devil's own job he had explaining sixteen pounds, eleven shillings and sixpence ha'penny, a small fortune at that time, located about his person. Luckily he'd had the sense to ditch the gun.

An Inspector of Books is waiting on the doorstep to carry out an audit. I chuckle to myself at his wasted journey—no power supply, no audit—only to discover the juice back on. No matter, nothing to hide.

I work in the public sector tourist industry looking after a cluster of ancient dwellings. Archaeological evidence favours a farming community. The village, such that it was, was abandoned when the descendants of its original inhabitants went off in search of a more comfortable lifestyle. Dropped everything and left. Of course it would help if we knew where they went. The pale Inspector makes small talk about the cold, but after being an hour on the hoof I'm sweating. I let him think it's my guilty conscience. I've nothing to hide. He produces his i.d. and I rummage around the bottom drawer for mine. Formalities over, I take his overcoat. Before I can do this, however, he must remove a pair of fleece lined leather gloves. I hang his coat; he throws hat and gloves on the table. He rubs his hands together. Where to begin? He looks around. It makes me shiver. I've seen his sort before. Once he picks up a scent there'll be no stopping him.

The audit itself is routine. He counts the money, takes readings from the till, sends me burrowing into boxes of stored files, makes copious notes, demands records of financial transactions over a targeted period and asks for a coffee to warm the cockles. When I return he's slipped off his navy jacket, loosened his tie and rolled up his sleeves like an engineer... or a jazz pianist, or like the unflinching auditor he is. My bottle of Jameson whiskey sits incriminatingly on the table before him.

'Will we celebrate the power supply coming back on?' he says. 'Eh? What do you say?'

'You know regulations forbid...' I say.

'We've had reports. Complaints you might call them.'

'I don't drink on duty if that's what you're saying.'

'Let's look at the evidence. Do you drink? Yes. This is your whiskey? Yes. Where was it concealed? In your desk. Back of the drawer. Handy for a snorter on a cold winter's day. Come on, I'm a man of the world.'

'I've said my bit. If it's my bottle at all you'll find the seal unbroken.'

He didn't stay for long. Not that he left with his tail between his legs. He made some minor criticisms, they always do, and confiscated my bottle of whiskey, but he forgot his gloves. Fleece lined leather gloves.

In the evening Alice drove down to meet me. It was a shock to see her and she was smiling. She said she'd given Riff-raff a lift home and also that she wouldn't want to see me struggling uphill in dwindling light. But I know her better than that. I know she wanted to gloat. To show me her capability with mechanical things and point out my want of any.

'Got her going then?' I blustered. 'Damp plugs? Thought so.'

'I thought that too, but no, Ralph tweaked something under the bonnet and she's been all right ever since.'

'Riff-raff?'

'Ralph. He's been a great help today, I don't know what I'd have done without him. He whitewashed the pantry for me. He said he couldn't leave it any longer like it was. You must remember to thank him when you see him next.'

'Didn't you read my note? I gave it another coat this morning.'

'Never mind it's done now. Ralph said it should last for years now.'

'Hey, by the way, I almost forgot. Here, for you. It's a pair of gloves. Not exactly what you need, but...'

'Gloves?' In the exchange a crude brown paper parcel I'd hastily put together began to unravel. She told me that a load of logs had been delivered soon after I left. She said that Riff-raff (Ralph) helped her stack them in the shed then he'd fixed the outside toilet and got the stove going. The house was warmer than it'd been all winter. Her voice trembled between expectation and lack of interest. She'd had a day of highs and was preparing herself for the inevitable low. 'But why gloves? Of all things.'

'You don't have any. And they're fleece-lined, warm as pie. Try them on. You can wear them anywhere. In the car driving or when you're out shopping. Anywhere. They're all the rage in town. Riff-raff'll like them. You can wear to bed if you like. Why not..?'

'His name's Ralph. Why won't you call him Ralph?'

Contributors

Maria Louse Apichella is a PhD candidate at Aberystwyth. She was shortlisted for the 2012 Bridport Prize. and published in *Scintilla, Magma, Visions of Life, the James Dickey Review* and *Love is the Law.*

Jean Atkin's 2012 pamphlet *The Dark Farms* from Roncadora Press was launched at Wigtown Book Festival. She is a previous winner of the Torbay Prize and the Ravenglass Poetry Prize. She has also published *The Treeless Region,* (Ravenglass Poetry Press 2010), and *Lost At Sea,* (Roncadora Press 2011).

David Batten taught poetry and creative writing, won the inaugural *Roundyhouse* poetry competition, been three times long/short-listed for the Cinnamon Press Poetry Award and published in *Envoi.* His fifteen minutes of poetic fame came when asked by Carol Ann Duffy to read a poem at her reading at Machynlleth. He lives in Aveyron, France.

Ron Carey lives in Dublin with his very supportive wife, Cathy. His poems have appeared in many magazines and anthologies in Ireland and the UK. In 2011 he was Highly Commended in the Bridport Prize and shortlisted in the Lightship Poetry Prize. He is studying for a Masters in Writing at Glamorgan University.

Jonathan Carr won second prize in the 2012 Fish Short Story contest, judged by David Mitchell. He has contributed many travel articles to Greece's *Athens News* and won the 'Greene and Heaton' prize on Bath Spa's MA in Creative Writing course. He lives in Italy.

Gina Challen lives in Sussex with her dog, Timmy. She had a midlife crisis in 2009 and went to study English and Creative Writing at the University of Chichester. In September she continues this wonderful madness with the start of a Masters in Creative Writing. 'Green Feathers' is her first published piece.

Anthony Costello is currently living in Brittany and working on a second poetry collection called *Dreaming Tigers*. His poetry has appeared in the following magazines: *Fire, Anon, Orbis, Magma, DreamCatcher, Poetry Review (UK)*.

Stuart Duncan has been a professional stand up comedian, but since taking a degree in Creative Writing and Literature, has focussed on poetry and fiction. *Bar Code* is forthcoming with Anarchy Books.

Lindsay Fursland has been published in *Stand* magazine, winning their first international poetry competition. He is Stanza rep for Cambridge, where he helps arrange poetry readings for the organisation CB1.

Jacci Garside published in several poetry magazines, including *Acumen, Iota, Fourteen, Other Poetry, Obsessed with Pipework, New Writer*, three Cinnamon Press anthologies, and a Flarestack Poets anthology. Enjoys performing poetry and is working hard to produce a first collection.

Chloe George lives in Hackney, and works full time as an online editor for a charity. She's just started writing short stories and her first one was published in *Front View* in November 2012.

Sarah Hegarty's short fiction has been published in *Mslexia,* the *Momaya Annual Review* and placed in competitions. Her first novel, *The Ash Zone*, won the 2011 Yeovil Literary Prize, and she is working on her second novel. She lives in Guildford with her family.

Janet Holst is a New Zealander currently living in Oman. She has taught in Melanesia, New Zealand, South Africa and the Middle East. Her stories have been published in South Africa and Australia, and academic articles in various journals.

Helen Holmes took an MA in Creative Writing at Newcastle University. One of her short stories won a New Writing North competition; others have been shortlisted for Cinnamon Press, *Mslexia,* The Fine Line and Lightship competitions. Her work appears in four anthologies. Helen lives in North Northumberland.

David Keyworth has written poetry regularly for ten years, published in *The SHOp, Smiths Knoll, Orbis* and elsewhere. He has poems in a previous Cinnamon anthology – *Feeding the Cat* and won the poetry category in Salford University's WriteNorthWest competition.

Kelvin M. Knight lives in Cumbria and is an advocate of the short story. He has previously had stories published in *Writers' Forum* magazine and writes reviews for *Albedo1* magazine. In 2012, he started a creative writing MA at Northumbria University. He is working towards his first anthology of short stories, *Love I Am.*

Gillian Laker was born in Hong Kong and lives in Kent where she belongs to the SaveAs writers group. Her poems have appeared on the *Guardian* website and in various anthologies, including Cinnamon's *In the Telling.* Her work was shown within a multi-media exhibition held in Odense, Denmark.

Phil Madden is working on a book about 'Paths' with the engraver Paul Kershaw, about 'Puppets' with the engraver Peter Lazarov and a book about the Japanese Tea Ceremony, in between being angry with the government.

Jane McLaughlin poems have been widely published in magazines and anthologies, including several Cinnamon Press publications. She won the Cinnamon Press Writing Award in November 2010 for her story *A Roof of Red Tiles.* She lives in London and works as a freelance in further education and academic publishing.

Sylvia Moody is a psychologist, translator and writer. She has translated history and biography from Modern Greek, written books on dyslexia in adulthood and on ancient Greek philosophy, and also children's stories and adult fiction.

Sue Moules poems have appeared in three Cinnamon anthologies. Her most recent publications are *In the Green Seascape* (Lapwing, 2009) and *The Earth Singing* (Lapwing, 2010).

David Olsen's third poetry chapbook, *Sailing to Atlantis*, is forthcoming from Finishing Line Press in 2013. Earlier chapbooks were *New World Elegies* (2011) and *Greatest Hits 1983-2000* (2001). His work has appeared in dozens of British and American journals

Eluned Rees has travelled widely. She did an MA in Creative Writing in Bath and has published a number of poems. Last summer she spent time at Edinburgh Zoo as Writer in Residence. She works as a Cognitive Hypnotherapist and is currently writing a novel.

Patrick Riordan is married with three grown children. He studied fine art at Winchester and lives in Stroud where he works with adults with learning difficulties. He has published in various literary magazines. His story 'Parabola' was featured in *Storm at Galesburg* (Cinnamon Press).

Marg Roberts writes poetry and prose. She leads creative writing workshops and groups in residential homes and was Warwick's Poet Laureate 2009-10. She lives in Warwickshire, loves her family, cycling and reading of all kinds. She's worked as a shop assistant, waitress, teacher and, most recently, probation officer.

Kayley Roberts was born in Caernarfon and raised bilingually; she is interested in the concepts of language and environment, which crop up often in her poetry along with ideas on dreams, emotions and time travel. She aims to complete a PhD on the Russian formalist poets.

Michelle Shine's short fiction has appeared in *Grey Sparrow, Liars League, London* and *Epiphany*. Her debut novel *Mesmerised* is due to be published in 2013. She has an MA in Creative Writing from Birkbeck University, and is a proud member of Nomads writing group and the London Writer's Cafe.

Derek Sellen lives in Canterbury and writes poems, plays and short stories. His poems in this anthology come from a sequence, 'Sexual Histories', (not as exciting as its title) which extends from Alexander the Great to Profumo and the Moors murders.

Aisling Tempany has appeared in four previous Cinnamon Press anthologies since 2009, as well as recently appearing in the Templar Press anthology *Bliss*. She lives in Wales, and is studying part-time as a postgraduate in Swansea University, writing on Irish Modernists.

Nicola Warwick writes poetry and short fiction and has had work in various magazines, as well as being a finalist or shortlisted in previous Cinnamon Press Writing Awards. She lives and works in Suffolk.

Noel Williams is widely published in anthologies and magazines, including *Iota*, *Envoi*, *The North* and *Wasafiri* and has won many prizes. He has an MA in creative writing from Sheffield Hallam University where he's also a lecturer. He's co-editor of *Antiphon* magazine (antiphon.org.uk) and reviews editor for *Orbis*.

Martin Willitts, Jr. retired as a Senior Librarian in upstate New York. He is a visual artist of Victorian and Chinese paper cutouts. He was nominated for 5 *Pushcart* and 2 *Best Of The Net* awards. He has 23 chapbooks and 3 books of poetry including *Playing The Pauses In The Absence Of Stars* (Main Street Rag), and *No Special Favors* (Green Fuse).

Margaret Wilmot was born in California, M.W. studied at UC Berkeley before spending various years in the Mediterranean. She has lived in Sussex since 1978. 'Writing, for me, is a tool for making connections and refining perception—a search…'